Across the Water

Grace Ingoldby, the daughter of an English father and a Canadian mother, was educated in England and Belgium. When she married, she went to live in Northern Ireland and studied at Queen's University, Belfast. She reviewed for the magazine *Fortnight* and worked for the BBC, reviewing books on radio. Now thirty-six, with two children, she lives in Wiltshire and reviews for the *New Stateman*. She has recently completed her second novel.

Grace Ingoldby

Across the Water

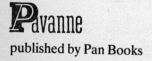
published by Pan Books

First published 1985 by Michael Joseph Ltd
This Pavanne edition published 1986 by Pan Books Ltd
Cavaye Place. London SW10 9PG
9 8 7 6 5 4 3 2 1
© Grace Ingoldby 1985
ISBN 0 330 29119 X

Printed in Great Britain by
Richard Clay (The Chaucer Press) Ltd,
Bungay, Suffolk

This book is sold subject to the conditions that it
shall not. by way of trade or otherwise. be lent. re-sold,
hired out. or otherwise circulated without the publisher's prior
consent in any form of binding or cover other than that in which
it is published and without a similar condition including this
condition being imposed on the subsequent purchaser.

We cannot withdraw our cards from the game. Were we as silent and as mute as stones, our very passivity would be an act.

> Jean-Paul Sartre
> *Presentation des Temps Modernes.*

Part One

The gates at the Big House, bloody great gates. A massive wrought-iron contortion of bizarre living creatures interlocked and on the move; a calculated interlacing of meandering curves which, inexorably, tortuously, connect. As a child they'd meant a lot to him. Beginning simply as the border of the world, a threshold one would never dare to cross alone, a limit and a barrier. As he grew older they became of course something to get beyond and to come back through, something to be shut properly, something to climb right to the very top of and shout. And, at one stage, I suppose it was at about the age of eleven, before he went across the water to school in England, they had, quite unexpectedly, explained themselves; his eyes had been able to discern and his mind to understand, not simply a series of whorls, but protruding tongues, the heads of snakes and leaping fish, the elongated bills of impossible ducks; heads in mouths and tails that wrap, wrap, around shoulders and he felt at once then that he was their equal and that he would trace them with a finger grown enormous in a dream . . . but the gates are over six feet tall and when he was old enough to reach them in comfort the moment of understanding had gone, had sunk again, had disappeared.

Although they now hang awkwardly from the massive stone gate posts that are popular there, and bits somehow have been broken off, gone missing and lost forever in the tumultuous growth of that summer of '76, they were once under some protection order and a tiny grant was proffered for their upkeep; but either the letter suggesting this had never arrived or had been mislaid in the womanless panic of the house, or perhaps the grant, like so much that summer, just unexpectedly, dried up. Still they stood and the red cat slithered through them going in the opposite direction to Boyle, still 'the young Mr Hamilton' at forty odd, stooping, one hand on the iron work, the other on the handlebars of his bike. He leant there for a moment catching his breath and then pushed on past the red plastic milk crate thrown over by someone, the Texaco drums peppered with air gun pellets that had arrived in the same way, over the wall, and lay now almost buried in the grass. Above him the sky was glorious with early morning sunshine, the sort of nine am that doesn't break its promise of a fine, dry day. He had pedalled quickly back from the island, furiously, because he had waited an hour for that bastard, that . . . he had waited an hour for a friend, that's all, a friend and he hadn't shown up.

As he stood like this for just that moment the sounds of nature rose in the quiet of the morning. A general underground hum of creatures on the wing and in the grasses, the regular pull and munch of cattle beside him in the Well field, the 'phut' of an old Massey tractor, rooks . . . He would still his ears against it, the heavy fecundity of that summer. He would shut it out, deny it. All was movement and life and flowers that hadn't bloomed for years now double-headed and enormous. He stooped once more to his bicycle and pushed on up the grassy drive, pushed on up to the house.

The joys of nature? Years ago, yes. Poking his nose into bird's nests, eggy blue, streaky colours; he'd pressed wild flowers between sheets of blotting paper. It only worked with flat-faced flowers, the juice would run out of the big ones, stain the absorbent paper like plasma, seep out and form a hard-edged ring. He'd made pictures from the flowers and his mother would say: 'Ach would you look at Boyle's dainty wee picture!' and his father, not at all keen on anything either dainty or wee would wander off and out, 'Tcch!' the noise in his throat of irritated disappointment.

Flower-pressing? Quite a gas. He hadn't made the connection then that to preserve flowers one had to kill them first.

His father was in the kitchen when he should by rights have been out, for there was a routine to their days together, some order. Dada, a great big man:

'A great man for the water so he is.'

'Swimming out there in the lake.'

Dada. Curled moustaches, clean, pared, fingernails, unpolished brogues, good shoes with broken laces, old cords and the comic strip sweater unravelling at the neck and at the ribbing so that if one twirled him May-day style he might just end up with sleeves. He swam out, two, three times a day, strong-hearted, seventy, his own man.

'Sure he might take an attack at any time. The old boy.'

And the kitchen in a mess. The red cat that he could have sworn he just passed, lay dozing in the fruit bowl that had long forgotten all about fruit, remembered only the feel of fur.

'You're back then?' said Dada, 'And your wee friend didn't show?'

The sink was full of dirty crocks and Boyle had to pour water through the spout of the kettle, his father moved, but only slightly, to let him near the cooker.

'He wouldn't show, I'd say,' said Dada watching his son, standing by the wireless, his place.

'Why's that?'

Dada had his hand on the knob of the wireless as if controlling the wave lengths by his grasp, 'Crawford Ferguson got it last night.'

Boyle looked at his father and back at the kettle; it didn't always whistle.

'Oh it was in the back parlour . . .' sang his father the big feet going in the music hall patter. 'His wife. What's that you call the old doll? Betty? Aye, poor wee Betty. Came running out to the parlour when the beasts started kicking up.'

'When?'

'Last night. It was on the nine o'clock, there now.'

The kettle boiled sending a shower of water shooting through the spout and out sizzling onto the range. His

9

father twiddled the moustache. He put his finger and his thumb just beneath his nose and then smoothed them outwards above his full, wide, mouth. Boyle made the tea, shaking the leaves into the pot.

'You'll be going into town then,' said Boyle.

'Aye.'

Boyle sat quiet, his father took his tea standing up. He could visualise it. Dada in the town and the town, Thursday, Mart day, bars overflowing like the kettle.

'And there's this,' said Dada, master dramatist, putting down his cup and holding a letter in his hand like he held on to the wireless, keeping information to himself.

'Oh.'

'Desmond.'

'Well?' Boyle's heart thumped. Desmond was his younger brother. They didn't hear from Desmond. Only about him. He was doing well across the water. One of the Hamiltons had made it. 'Will he be over?'

'Not at all. He's sending Aimee, the wife and the boy.' He looked down at the letter. 'Aimee and Jack. Jack and Jill went up the hill'.

'May I see it, the letter?'

'Surely,' but Boyle had to get up and take the letter from him, from his hand.

A routine to this house, some order . . . Boyle 'worked' in the dining room with the curtain on one window partly drawn. He heard his father back the Vauxhall; he stayed put for most of the morning for, over the years and by default, the dining room had become his place. The table, covered, twenty, thirty years before, in a brief fit of enthusiasm with carpet felt to protect it, held the story of Boyle's life in the house, Boyle's life.

A box of Derwent coloured pencils, stamp corners, binoculars, files and ring binders, magnifying glass, typewriter ribbons, index card system, water-colour paper, reproductions of Irish illuminated manuscripts cut from periodicals and magazines, books: art, ancient history, poetry, Milton and his mother's set of Mazo de la Roche, moral notions and the structure of reality, archaeology, architecture, archaic traditions and beliefs, stone carving in Fermanagh. By and in and around the fireplace was his latest interest: piles of newspapers, a great stack! Glue, scissors, tape, scrap books, and on the table now in front of him a sharpened pencil, his fountain pen, paper. Pulling the typewriter towards him he wrote yesterday's date and put: 'Crawford Ferguson, Rossbawn'.

He'd a new silage clamp Boyle remembered, for they were almost neighbours in this scarcely populated district. He had a new clamp and was doing all right, and it wasn't easy to do all right down here for Fermanagh is a wet, poor county in the North west of Ireland, the lakes running through it like a giant's ink spill; bright blue on the map from Pettigo to Newtown Butler, the ground a sodden scrub of reeds and rushes, blown thorn trees, heather skimmed on rock. Crawford would be about fifty-one, and the bullet entered his head. How does the body fall, he wondered? And if you're shot in the head, does the blood spurt or trickle, does it gush? 'And you?' he thought of Sean his friend. No he would tackle one thing at a time. Not that his brain was inadequate, no, not like a man who fails at chess because he cannot anticipate, premeditate or plan, but because this was the way he carried himself, this was the way he held himself together just now. Like a piece of porcelain broken in several places, he was, as they say in those parts, 'wired-up'. His mind held the murder of Ferguson, the forthcoming visit of Aimee and Jack and the non-appearance of the boy, his friend, Sean; separate incidents he would not confuse by synthesis.

The boy. Boyle turned the notion of the boy in his mind, a friend and everybody needs a friend. A quick, quiet boy, different religion, different background and the most important difference being that Sean was young, enthusiastic, unbattered, complete, as much the future as Boyle felt himself to be the past. He thought perhaps of walking across to Sean's farm now, but no, he wouldn't do it. How typical the tender trap, he thought, drawing circles on the carpet felt that didn't show up.

Loyalty?

'I'll meet you right by the stone Mr Hamilton.'

No. He had been betrayed.

The radio played on in the empty kitchen, the gates swung open, an army landrover pulled up on the grassy gravel sweep beyond the closed front door.

Captain Mark Robbins was on his third tour, unscathed but increasingly superstitious. In Dungannon, in '72, he had got out of his vehicle to check on a house they had just passed. He sometimes did this, his mother had an interest in Irish architecture, listed buildings generally, and he always checked things out for her, made a mental note to describe later in a letter. The vehicle had gone a little further up the road with the idea of pulling into a farm gateway where it would not cause an obstruction. It drove on without him, over a culvert bomb detonated by remote control from several fields away. Fate. His non-presence in the vehicle with his men had been difficult to explain to his commanding officer but the senior man had heard him out and understood, stopped him in fact in mid-flow. For Robbins had been lucky and whatever it was that protected or appeared to protect you, the heather stuck behind the tax disc, the detail that kept you back in barracks that vital minute more, whatever it was, the finer points were best left hanging, safer not gone over, for luck evaporated should it be explained away.

Now, on a probably fruitless expedition following up the death of Ferguson the night before, Robbins stood before the Big House and looked it over for his ma. Typically Irish, he would write, falling down around their ears. By the look of the crack which ran the length of the gable wall it appeared to be falling outwards, like Ireland itself, an inner rot, internal combustion, once gracious and now God forsaken.

'Morning. Lovely set of gates you've got there,' he said

introducing himself as Boyle finally opened up at the second, third knock. 'Sorry for the intrusion, not having lunch I hope?'

'Lunch?'

Boyle came out and shut the door protectively behind him, shading his eyes against the brightness of the day.

Robbins explained his purpose. Ferguson, last night about six-thirty, no car yet, might have used a boat, seen or heard anything useful?

The stooping man was almost familiar he thought, gaunt, pale-faced, he looked shocked. Well it was shocking all of it. He made a signal to his troops, several soldiers got out, guns in their hands.

'All right if we take a look about, a recce?'

Boyle nodded.

He watched the soldiers spread about the place, some to the back to the byres and sheds, others to the foot of the hilly garden to poke their guns uselessly into the bank of rhododendrons. So many people about, he thought, so suddenly.

Robbins looked about him, his glance taking in the old lead gutterings sprouting greenery, the flower beds gone to hell, the broken paving and the crumbling wall from which stone steps led down to what once must have been a well kept and gracious lawn. His thoughts turned to tennis and croquet, he watched his men, teenagers, in the garden with their guns. Crossing to the landrover he reached down a clipboard from the passenger seat.

'You and your father here?'

'Yes.'

'Is your father about?'

'He is not.'

Boyle stood close to the house, he'd seen the officer's wandering eyes and he felt as if he wanted to protect it all, the house, the garden, shield it, cover it with a cloth from prying foreign eyes.

'Sorry about this,' repeated Robbins, still finding the man familiar, still unable to place him. 'Cigarette?'

Boyle shook his head.

'Have you got a boat here?'

'It's not used.'

'May I take a look?'

'Surely.' Boyle led the man down the steps into the garden, over the humpy lawn and down along an almost hidden path through the leaping rhododendrons to a small open boathouse. Inside an old clinker boat with a ragged piece of tarpaulin covering the inboard engine, several pairs of oars against the wall of the house.

'Thank you.'

Obviously the boat had not been used this season, probably for years.

'Well.' They turned and walked back up the garden. With Boyle walking in front of him, a stooping walk, the picture clicked for Robbins all at once.

'Hamilton!' he exclaimed. 'I knew it rang a bell. You're Boyle Hamilton and you've a brother, Derek?'

'Desmond.'

'Good God!' Robbins put his hand to his forehead and removed his cap.

'Mark Robbins,' he said, delighted by the coincidence that had brought them so oddly together. 'I remember you. Do you remember me?'

'I do, surely,' Boyle shook the soldier's hand.

'By God!' said Robbins, 'I thought I knew the face.'

'I didn't recognise you at all.'

'Now hang on,' said Robbins, he sat down on the top step thinking.

'It's all coming back now. You,' he spoke slowly, remembering. 'You were older. Right? You left early . . . your mother . . .'

'Yes.'

'So what happened to Desmond?'

'Desmond stayed over, in England.'

'Did he? What's he up to?'

'He writes plays.'

'Honestly!'

'He does. He has a play on in London now.'

'My God!' Robbins shook his head. 'I'm posted here,' he said, 'in Enniskillen. Three months. We ought to see something of each other.'

His troops came up the garden still holding their weapons, indicating that there was nothing.

He motioned for them to get back into the vehicle, he sat on. 'A small world indeed,' he said. 'And your father? Is he still going strong?'

Boyle nodded.

'And Dessie, does he come over much?'

'No.'

'Pity.'

'His wife's coming,' remembered Boyle, 'they have a child. You're not married yourself?'

'No. And you?'

'No.'

'I'd like to see Dessie again,' said Robbins. 'In any case we two must get together.' He got up now, touched Boyle on the arm. 'I am sorry we had to meet this way. This one,' he indicated the murder on the clipboard, 'a little close to home.'

Boyle made no comment.

'I'd like to come out, socially if I may.'

'Oh yes, of course, for an evening, I could telephone the barracks.'

'No. Look, don't worry, don't do that. I'll be around for a bit sorting this lot out. If I may I'll just drop in. If that's all right with you?'

'Of course.'

'Give my regards to Dessie if you hear from him. I suppose if his wife's coming he might turn up?'

'He might.'

'Fine. Well. I'll be out of your way anyway for a while at least,' he shook hands once again, always shaking hands, thought Boyle, always apologising. 'A nasty business,' he was saying as he held the clipboard in a strong brown hand, a signet ring on his little finger, 'one thing . . .'

'Yes?'

'The people on the other side of you, Maguires,' he looked down at the board.

'Yes?'

He turned to a map covered in perspex.

'Just the other side of us. There.' Boyle marked the spot with a guilty finger.

'No Mr Maguire,' Mark consulted his notes, 'three sons, wife, Roman Catholic, small farm . . .'

'You have it all there.'

'We'll go and take a look see I suppose.' Mark leant into the vehicle and gave directions to his driver, the headphones crackled within. Once again he surveyed the house, thinking it a dreadful shame.

'A very fine pair of gates you've got there,' he said by way of compensation.

'They are. If you would be sure to pull them to . . .'

'Of course. Well. I'll be seeing you.'

Boyle stood back against the closed front door. He nodded. The captain replaced his cap, they drove off, the soldier at the back squatting on his haunches, his machine gun cutting a black stripe in the lunchtime sun. Mark saw to it that the gates were properly shut, mulled over the house, the strange coincidence.

'You know him then sir?' said one of his men.

'I do actually. At school with him, and his brother.'

'That's a turn up,' said the soldier.

'Yes.' Strange how these things happen, he pondered as they drove out along the quiet, empty roads again, it would be good to see Dessie again. Boyle was a bit dreary, a square peg really, but Dessie was all right. He hadn't known Boyle so well, he was older and age mattered at school rather. Funny how it all came back, Boyle had left under a bit of a cloud, something about, what was it, a pair of study curtains going up in smoke . . . How strange! The Irish at school had more trouble fitting in than the chaps from Kenya, Nigeria. No flies on Dessie now though, plays on in London. Still, the Irish were like that, still waters, a lot of them had a gift for it. The sun was warm through the open side of the vehicle, Mark turned this thoughts briefly to the next port of call, Maguires. A routine investigation, they'd hardly come up with much. A close lot these people no matter which foot they kicked with. His other tours, Derry, Dungannon, rain, rain, rain. With the Hamiltons close too and in this sunshine things wouldn't be so bad perhaps. Of course one had nerves, he thought, instructing the driver to turn off now down a white concrete farm track. Each time it got worse, naturally one didn't say so but it was the case. Like the weather one wondered if one's luck would hold.

And Boyle, stirred so unexpectedly by the coincidence, by the intrusion, he gardened because now he had to do something, absolutely had to.

How? How had this come about? What had happened? The house, the garden, doors, windows, chimneys, water pipes, ivy, moss, weeds, weeds, buttercups, daisies, scutch grass, nettles, saplings, not a patch of bare earth . . .?

Of course there was a lot to do! Well, he'd just start here, now. He remembered this little bed, his mother's special bed. There used to be . . . hollyhocks and Canterbury Bells, tall, old-fashioned flowers, they flourished against this south-facing wall. He scrabbled at the earth with his fingers and knelt on something hard, parting the grasses he pulled hard at it. There you see! A grey, scalloped edging stone. He remembered those. He'd need a kitchen spoon, he'd need a trowel, the weeds, the nettles were embedded. The ground was dry as dust, it broke his nails; anyway no one could say he wasn't trying, it didn't matter how hard it was he would do it, starting here! There was a white flower too, she grew a white flower. Fairy's hair! He vividly remembered now the packets of seeds his mother bought: 'Gypsophilia Elegans, Covent Garden White' and she kept them in the kitchen drawer!

He wouldn't have it, no he really wouldn't have it. That look of pity on the soldier's face. The house was all right, nothing drastic, and he'd just get this flower bed cleared, and plant seeds, make what they call a 'nice show' . . . there was nothing wrong with the house! A few small jobs, that he would admit, and . . . he would get this bed done. Not a matter of surgery, only cosmetics. God, his mother! It must have upset her, how frustrating! Not being able to get out into the garden or see this little bed . . .

He came back on the boat to care for her, that was just after the curtain incident at school. It was Desmond's fault but he had taken the blame for it, the way Desmond had explained it seemed to have substance at the time, that put the hat on it, the curtains, they sent him back. They said that although he had the ability to take the Oxbridge exams that it was inadvisable 'at this stage'. They talked of mature students settling in very well. The school doctor had sent a letter to the doctor in Enniskillen: that he was in an unbalanced state due to being away from home and that this was exacerbated by his mother's condition. That the other brother was coping quite well but that it would be better all round for Boyle to return, rest a little, get his strength back, perhaps a tutor, a local man . . . If only I'd had a study of my own, thought Boyle working at the weeds. Even in the heat the thought of school made him shiver. The horror of it. A barn of a place, everything strange, everything unexplained, unwritten laws, a foreign code. If he'd had the study . . . but of course one was never alone at school, only in bed, and perhaps not even then.

Boyle sat back on his haunches and rubbed his eyes behind his glasses: 'Got to stop. Got to stop,' he said.

In the kitchen he washed his hands.

'Come along now, come along now,' and then hurried up the stairs to his bedroom and closed the door. 'Oh God! Oh God!'

He lay fully dressed under the bedclothes and tried like a child to think of something nice. Not Ferguson's blood or the soldiers' guns, not the streaked red of peonies or the break of stems, not Desmond, not Sean, not his mother, not Dada, not Aimee . . . and then he thought of his nephew, the little boy. A child in the house! They would play, what would they play? With a ball. Teach the child how to catch and how to hit a ball . . . and books, children's books; dinosaurs and space men, a child in the house.

He slept away the afternoon but his sleep was as thin as muslin bags. Through it the brown water lapped and gurgled, washed about him, pulsed and swelled. The line of straggling purple rhododendrons was mirrored in the surface of the water, it tilted, he wasn't quite sure then which was reflection, which was which.

He got himself downstairs, filled the kettle once again. His father swayed in the room like an enormous ragged tree. He wanted to talk, kicked the cat off the chair with the toe of his boot, wiped his moustaches with his fingers.

'Come on ya wee cub,' he said, 'Can you not speak to a man when he comes home? Nothing to say? And you footering about all day. Tchh! We'll have to get this place red up, red up!' raising his voice, a look at the overloaded sink and draining board. 'Gardening is it now? You're good for nothing when you could be helping me.'

'Helping you what?'

'With the cattle.'

Boyle sighed.

'I suppose you'll be out with your flower basket like the old doll?'

Boyle stretched across the table for his book, keeping silent, keeping the peace.

'Can you not be a man Boyle? Is there something wrong in there?' asked Dada putting his hard finger to his son's forehead. 'You're a wee bit daft perhaps, is that it?'

The kettle did its spluttering act and Boyle tried to get to it but his father kept him in his seat.

'Come on,' he said, 'I want to hear it. Talk, talk, damn you, little bastard.'

'The troops were here checking on Maguires.'

'Not before time, cowboys!'

'They came here.'

'To the house?'

'They searched the garden, looked at the boat.'

Dada digested this information and allowed Boyle to make the tea. 'So you're tidying it up for those uns are you?' he said taking his cup.

'Of course not.'

Ferguson's death was mentioned again on the evening news, no longer headlines. Boyle could, if he had cared to, imagine the scene just across the fields. The spotless kitchen and the faces that would later be described as 'stricken'; the cups of tea, the cigarettes in shaky, unaccustomed hands, the medicinal tots of whisky. The plans for the funeral already under way, relatives to be sent for from England and America, the farm to be taken care of, the insurance. 'Mr Ferguson met his death' that's what the papers would say, as if there was time in a shooting incident for some greeting, some recognition. Boyle thought of this fearful moment; he saw it existing in a timeless way but shied away from it like a horse that suspects a paper bag blown from the hedge.

They sat in silence smoking. Years of wet weather had done little so far to alter the pattern of their lives. Outside the air was still warm and buzzing. Flies skimmed the surface of the lake where the red cat stalked, far away now, overseeing his territory: a sleek opportunist, a little king.

Dada wrote to Desmond, a perfunctory letter saying he would be glad etc, time of arrival. He didn't say much to Boyle but it was obvious he was excited, fidgeting about, folding and re-folding the newspaper, banging his pipe against the leg of the chair. Boyle switched on the light and read of the great heroes. Passionate men, bigger than his father. Men now almost lost in the labyrinth between fantasy and fact, history and myth. Cuchulain and his seagoing chariot, men brave to the point of foolhardiness. Men together, not like at school.

'I know your thoughts,' he read, 'for we have slept under the one cloak and drunk from the one wine cup.'

The softness of hard men.

He turned from his book to look through the uncurtained window into the darkness, to think of the boy he had waited so long for on the island and of the little boy who was coming, his nephew, the child.

Desmond waved his wife and child goodbye but did not see them off. Passengers for Northern Ireland were segregated at the airport, sent off with their belongings to a separate pre-departure lounge. Desmond, Irish expert at the local pub where the Hamiltons leased a cottage, had been no more aware of this security measure than his attractive English wife. Thus their parting – and what had he anticipated after all – waving at the plane? the face at the window? Jack's face – was swift, formal and for Desmond perhaps a mite embarrassing.

As he drove back into London, his suitcase, his London clothes in the back of the car, he pondered, wordsmith that he was, what it was exactly that Heathrow, the clawing arm of Northern Ireland, had denied him then, for he felt, he tossed the words, disquieted, somehow uneasy. He had manipulated this latest parting as easily as he combed his thinning reddish hair. He could justify it on several counts if called to do so, what mattered was that it was necessary for him. His latest play, *Here Today*, the story of a modern-day Florence Nightingale wading in the horror of Saigon, her attempts to adopt an orphaned Vietnamese, was in rehearsal at the Kings Head Islington; Bernie, a mate had come up trumps with the London flat again, the sun shone and the living at last was easy. So a lucky man, he should have been quite happy, and as the day progressed, he persuaded himself that he was.

Aimee left Heathrow with the mixed emotions of Oates leaving the shaky security of Scott's tent. Oates came from Enniskillen, Desmond had told her that, the place meant nothing to her but the journey did.

At first she had been apprehensive, leaving mother, leaving England, taking Jack on her own into the blue. Desmond had prattled on during the drive to the airport, talk of another holiday, later on and somewhere else, leaving him did not distress her, leaving mother, now that they had once again grown close, preoccupied her during the drive but she had put that behind her now. She had left her mother before of course and never more disastrously than the day she had married Desmond at the registry office in South Kensington almost seven years before. Marrying Desmond had been about leaving her mother, Aimee knew that now. Desmond had adored her briefly, and briefly she had adored the adoration of it all. She deserved to be adored, her father had taught her that, she deserved to be cherished for the neat ankles, the little wrists, it had hurt to be so hastily abandoned because of the equally diminutive proportions of her mind. It was all against Mummy, she bitterly regretted it now. Desmond's admiration had mesmerized her like a snake. Now she knew, or at least suspected, that these days he slithered and sloughed his freckly skins elsewhere. It was insulting but she'd got over it, she knew nothing about the theatre, didn't really see the point, the role of second fiddle, playwright's wife, did not appeal to her nature which was, always had been, that of first violin.

Jack sat on her lap, excited but sleepy in the heat. Her travelling companion, an accountant who looked like a farmer over whom Jack had earlier spilt his orange squash had asked her where she was going, had told her that it was a beautiful part of the world altogether, talked to her about the lakes. Aimee slipped graciously from the conversation, pretended to concentrate on Jack's wrigglings, at the cloud banks beyond the window on her left. Beautiful or not, lakes, no lakes, it was sufficient just to go.

'How ghastly!' her mother had said when they'd discussed it, 'Are you sure you really want to go?'

'You'll love it!' Desmond had told her, 'You know you hate London in the heat.'

Aimee couldn't remember whether she hated London hot or cold but she hadn't bothered this time to argue or to protest. Like Scott's men she saved her energy these days, like Oates she had weighed the pros and cons.

The accountant caught her eye and smiled at her, she was attractive and she knew she was, too good for the likes of him. Desmond had his plays, mother had her garden, she had brought Jack up on her own in that rotten borrowed cottage, she had got her figure back; like the plane she saw herself to be breaking through a bank of clouds, she was glad to get away. It was thus almost with elation that she returned the accountant's smile, agreed with him that Jack was big for his age and gorgeous with it, it couldn't matter less.

It took an hour, the journey, and like much else in Aimee's recent past she perceived it, the indignity of being searched, the annoyance of having to share a seat with Jack, as something like a minor but necessary operation, that she acquiesced to undergo. Aimee did not talk to strangers but if she had she might have said that, no, she wasn't worried by 'The Troubles' and that actually she had left and was arriving with a calm but empty heart. She hadn't argued with her husband, had not even bothered to put up a defence. 'It isn't worth the candle anymore,' she'd say, 'it isn't worth the fight. I'm treading water in the sky if you must know,' she thought pleased with herself at last as they began their descent to land, scattering rabbits at Aldergrove airport where the sight of Dada, the figure of him, taller than the other men, claiming her and her son from the accountant at the luggage carousel brought her down to earth at last with a rather sudden and sickening jolt.

He hadn't changed for better or worse since the wedding, a big man with a knuckly grasp, a foreigner, her heart sank as he embraced her and the child. How was Dessie? how old would Jack be now? how was her mother? a lovely woman. Aimee shivered at the memory of her last meeting with this man, that awkward wedding, the series of absolutely unforgivable faux pas. But Dada was as pleased as punch, introduced her lavishly here and there. His daughter-in-law, Aimee, Dessie's wife, and Aimee smiled politely. 'Ach isn't that great,' they said.

Eventually her luggage came through and with it loaded on a trolley they went out, through more security to a small car park – that was it, the airport – a cluster of buildings, an open car park. She was baffled by the smallness of it, the overt army and police presence, the relaxed and accepting atmosphere.

'I suppose you get used to it,' she said.

'Ach you do surely.'

'I mean, it's not dangerous in Fermanagh? Where you are?'

'Not at all,' he said, 'Not at all.'

'Has it been very hot?' she'd asked and 'powerful' he'd replied, 'a fierce heat.' He talked like Desmond but somehow it was not as irritating coming from him. She offered to put Jack in the back of the car, he suggested that Jack ride in the front on her knee. Although she was against it she agreed.

The journey seemed a long one. He showed her the map but she didn't take it in. She didn't drive. Desmond had never encouraged her and it was just another of those things she had never got round to, and as a non-driver she could not have told you exactly where she was going or by what route she had come. She sat instead looking through the window as the car pottered through the countryside, looking out at fields and thinking them, too, small and shabby, in scale and tone with what she'd seen of the resident population.

After the motorway, a dual carriageway with bridges of which he was inordinately proud, they pursued circuitous diversions around towns and villages already bombed or rightly suspicious of being so. After the early formalities of greeting these two strangers drove on in silence, racketing over ramps constructed to slow them down, Jack slept as they went on and on, through Augher, Clogher, round Fivemiletown. A patrol stopped them, UDR explained Dada, locals he elaborated. 'Down from the airport', he told them, Aimee introduced again, Aimee smiling. Where on earth was she going, what was she doing here at all?

Through Eniskillen, built on a lake, as proud of this as he was of the motorway, out past the town, Jack still sleeping, along the fringes of the lake. Bugger Desmond for doing this to me, she thought as they drove through the open gates and into Ballyross.

Boyle thought there was something wrong with Jack, seeing him carried in. He was nervous, Aimee kissed him, walking behind her towards the kitchen he saw her little pink shoes with straps around the ankles, touched the place where she had kissed him with his fingers, like a child himself he watched her.

'Tea?' said Dada.

'Oh tea, surely. Will we take it in the kitchen there or the sitting room perhaps, I . . .'

'Please don't fuss on my account,' said Aimee. 'Kitchen's fine by me. One of the family please.'

'In the kitchen then,' said Boyle disappointed. 'You haven't changed Aimee, not a bit. You don't look a day older . . .'

'Older than what?' she laughed.

'I mean . . .'

'Thank you Boyle,' she said, her voice with a rise in it, like a teacher accepting a bunch of hopelessly short-stemmed flowers.

'Would the . . . would Jack like to go upstairs?'

'No. I'll keep him with me. If I put him down he'll only bawl. I would like to wash my hands?'

Boyle showed her the sink which mercifully and for once was empty.

She put the boy carefully in Dada's armchair, immediately he began to cry.

'Towel?'

'Certainly,' and Boyle raced upstairs. They didn't use a towel, a dish cloth they used. He returned with a towel, the child, looking about him, let out another loud wail.

'Oh dear,' said Boyle standing useless his arms at his sides.

Aimee picked up her son. 'He'll be all right,' she said,

25

'It's all strange to him.'

It was strange for Boyle, being kissed, a woman in the kitchen using a towel; she folded it and put it over the bar of the range, very naturally, folding it neatly, the child on her hip.

'He's a big boy.'

'Yes, I suppose he is rather.'

'A grand wee cub,' said Dada coming in.

Boyle stood aside. 'I'll make the tea then,' he said.

'Lovely.'

'You've a great heap of stuff there,' said Dada, a caressing humour in his voice that Boyle hardly recognised.

'Isn't it awful! It's children. One can't go anywhere without the kitchen sink!' Yet she didn't look as if she spent much time at the sink somehow. Her hands were small and soft, she wore nail varnish.

'It matches your shoes,' said Boyle.

'Sorry,' she looked blank.

'The polish, your nails.'

'Ach don't listen to him!' said Dada, 'daft as a brush,' but he said it lightly too, almost affectionately.

Boyle put the cups and saucers on the table. He had washed and dried them up himself, a sugar bowl and milk jug.

'This is some style,' commented his father. 'Will you take a drop of something in it? A wee whisky?'

'Not for me.'

'Would you like something to eat now?' asked Boyle.

Both men danced attendance.

'I never eat when I'm travelling.'

'Would you Jack?' asked Boyle speaking to the child for the first time but Jack hid his head in his mother's dress.

'Perhaps a bit of bread and butter,' said Aimee. 'Now, sit there Jack.' She put him on a chair beside her but he clung on. 'Come on, sit properly. I can't drink my tea with you on my lap, come on.' Jack sat alone but he didn't like it, his hand held hard to his mother. 'He sat on my lap all the way,' she explained. 'The lump! Quite exhausting. Shall I pour?' She put the tea in first and then added the milk.

Boyle watched spellbound. 'You had a good journey apart from that I mean?'

'Very quick,' she replied. 'Awfully hot! I thought it might be cooler over here.'

'Not a bit of it!' said Boyle.

'Ah now,' agreed his father, 'Ah now.'

'I must say it's further than I thought, from the airport to here.'

'A hundred miles,' claimed Dada as if he'd paced it out himself.

He drank his tea at a gulp. 'You take it easy now,' he said and rose to take the cases upstairs.

Aimee poured more tea, silently Boyle accepted another cup. Perhaps he's not a well man thought Aimee surveying Boyle's pallid anxious face and wondered why she was already slipping into the world of double negatives. Desmond spoke like that, 'not well' instead of ill. In the brief silence as she drank her tea she thought of him as if she'd left him a long time ago. His turn of phrase, the idioms of his speech which rose from the surface when he was angry or drunk. Desmond shouting, telling her to 'catch herself on', Desmond always 'parched' or 'moithered' for drink. She wondered if Boyle drank, most of them did. The world in the 1970s was smaller than ever before but the distance between England and Ireland remained, she thought, immense.

'How is Desmond?' asked Boyle who had spent the time making eyes at Jack and getting no response.

'Fine, marvellous, doing very well at the moment. Dreadfully busy of course.'

'Yes?' said Boyle waiting, wanting more.

'He told you about the play I suppose, he tells everyone about the play.'

'Yes.'

'And I think he may have something else up his sleeve.'

'Not a rabbit I hope,' said Boyle and giggled nervously.

Aimee smiled sweetly. I'm going to go bananas stuck

here, she thought. This is a mistake.

Dada returned, 'Still chatting away? Will you not show the lady to her room, and the young gentleman here.'

The young gentleman tried a smile and found it was not too difficult.

He led the way: 'Come on now. Up those stairs! Where are we now?' he queried as if ladies and gentlemen frequently came to stay.

'Aimee's in mother's room, here,' said Boyle opening the door.

The room was quiet and clean, Aimee's quick, starling glance took it all in.

'Lovely,' she said more than a little relieved. 'Thank you Boyle. And Jack?'

'Jack's here, just across the corridor. Your Daddy slept here,' he said to Jack.

Boyle opened the door onto a large bare room, the old nursery. The windows were long and came almost to floor level and looked out across the garden to the purple of the rhododendrons and the lake. Aimee was tired now, disappointed. But what had she expected? 'I think it's a little big for him.'

'The beds are wee,' said Boyle and sat on one to prove it. 'And bars on the windows you see, a great view altogether.' He bent down to touch the bars which came up to his knees. 'You see he couldn't fall from here.'

'It smells damp,' said Aimee.

Boyle and his father sniffed harmoniously. Dada opened one of the windows and Jack rushed across to look out.

'No. Jack, Jack! Come away from the window darling, Jack! Oh dear am I being frightfully difficult?' she said turning to them, 'I'm awfully silly about the damp.'

'He might take my room,' suggested Boyle.

'Oh no, I wouldn't dream of it,' Aimee gestured flat disbelief with her little hands.

'No please, it's nothing.' Boyle showed her down the bare corridor and across the landing to his own room, neat and tidy, small.

Aimee had a good sniff. 'Well it certainly smells more healthy. But really, no I couldn't . . .

'Please . . .'

'Not at all, I can move my stuff.'

'Well it really is very good of you,' they went back downstairs. No pictures observed Aimee, no flowers, so bare. 'One can't take any risks with damp . . .'

So Boyle took the room opposite Aimee. The old nursery with its memories of cots and medicines and Nellie with the blackheads who smacked them when they wet.

Dada took his daughter-in-law out for a drink, discarded his tie and waistcoat but did not yet see fit to return to the comfort of his unravelling jumper. They made quite a couple; she in the little pink shoes, her dress and cardigan, her handbag and sunglasses, away out in the Vauxhall that smelt of sheep.

Boyle was horrified about being left. Jack had gone straight to sleep and he had been instructed not to 'dash up' to him at the first cry. She seemed unconcerned about the child, perhaps it was a good child thought Boyle, he had no idea. In any case he sat for a while on the staircase after they had left and the crunch of the car on the gravel, the swing of the gates, had gone, leaving silence to seep back into the old house. Silence, but not the same old silence; Jack was sleeping upstairs, Dada and Aimee were coming back.

He made them sandwiches with egg but made the mistake of putting the mixture in warm so that the butter went waxy and hard. When the 'quick drink' turned into a long one, he remembered to cover the sandwiches. His mother had done that for Dada; she used a muslin cloth and although the curtains were made of similar stuff and he had thought momentarily of using a bit of them he settled eventually for an inverted plate. At eleven he listened to the news on the wireless, left the light on in the hall and went upstairs to bed. Out of habit he went to his own room and found the sleeping child, the bedclothes slipping sideways, half kicked off in the heat. Very, very gently he

29

covered him up and drew the curtains shutting out the stars and moon.

Jack slept, the lake noise entered his dreams in a steady, slow, relentless, rhythm, far away in London his father paced the floor. It had been a long day for daddy, a long day.

Rehearsals, begun that afternoon, had been fraught and with the temperature still in the 90s tempers were short. Desmond had changes to make, changes that, at this late hour, would have to wait for tomorrow. He'd expected it, these changes, he knew it would happen, it always did, so why, if one really learnt from one's experiences, why, did it annoy him now? Why did it fucking hurt? Theoretically plays were like children, influenced beyond the womb, they changed, altered, sometimes like children it might be better to disown them. To use his double negative Desmond had 'not been unprepared' but Roddy, the director, a smooth little wimp, really got up his nose.

'Why don't we try something a little closer to home next time,' he suggested, patronising bastard.

But Desmond had fought his corner, Desmond had stood up well. Two, three years ago he would have what, fallen on the Brontës and their like in the defence of his choice, Vietnam, insisted that one didn't actually have to experience everything first hand, that there existed such a thing as imagination. Now he simply lied to Roddy, told him that he was actually tackling Ireland and that Vietnam had been – and surely Roddy of all people could see the connections here, couldn't he? – had been a run-in for him. He didn't after all – and how he charmed Roddy, how he charmed him – want to capitalise, now did he? The situation in Ireland today was too terrible – Desmond had explained his position with an expression of deep, considered, concern – too cynically treated already, too complex altogether, to simply jump in there and do it. He wouldn't use Ireland, God's own country and all that, as a vehicle for something else, he had to wait, didn't he, on the old muse?

'My dear boy,' he'd told Roddy, for Roddy was a boy, an English boy like the boys at school, groomed for stardom and getting it, 'Wait and you shall see.'

Desmond relived this conversation without much comfort alone at Bernie's where he had taken to the drink. He'd tried it on with the girl who played Frances, the lead actress, the Florence of his imagination, but she didn't want to know. She was good though and that was comforting, the critics would pick her up; it would all be all right on the night. At ten they'd called it a day, he'd started drinking then for the theatre was above a pub, within one. The boys at home, round Ballyross, the lads he'd run with in the holidays, would think that a great laugh, a theatre in a pub, the right mix. He hoped it worked this time around for the weather was against him, too hot.

Sleepless, alone in London, a little drunk, Desmond felt his age and weary. Portobello had still been buzzing when he'd finally made his way back, life, vitality, so why now did he feel so sour, why did everything seem so stale? In the old days, his first time, the play about school days which had knocked the wankers he had hated but so cleverly used, right down in the aisles, London had been a magic city then. And Bernie's flat, Nirvana! Late '60s, early '70s, perhaps it was his own age at this time? Then it seemed to him that the streets of London were indeed paved with gold. Up in Notting Hill, Portobello, with its swirl of cultures, had epitomized for him everything that was the present, everything he needed to obliterate his past. Here, a dozen, half a dozen years ago, he'd felt that he had at last got his just deserts, that he had at last emerged from the Dark Ages and found himself fit, fighting and on his feet. These people, the Rastas, the Greeks, Nigerians, West Indians, even the Irish in Hammersmith and Cricklewood, these were the people he would be writing for and about: '70s people, moving people, optimism flashed across the sky. There existed, or so he perceived it then, a possibility of social mobility unhampered by colour, class, education, background or religion. A new world unfettered by the chains that brought down Ulster. Power to the people?

Bathed in sweat and the orange glow that keeps night alive in London, Desmond lay in bed examining these memories, old feelings, without affection for he could not, would not bear to feel a fool. As sleep came to him at last an unsought phrase of Ibsen's spoken in Roddy's recently acquired non-accent, rose up to roll with him all night. 'We sail with a corpse in the cargo, eh Desmond, eh?'

London had never been hotter. Blackout curtains were hung at office windows, merchant bankers dug out ancient T.A. shorts, Denis Howell was appointed Minister for Drought.

Desmond, priding himself on his professionalism under strain (mornings writing with a hangover) tailored his new play for the previews, tucked it in at the waist, gave more style to the shoulders, more fullness to the skirt. A temporary synthesis emerged between writer, director, cast, stage management, *Here Today* opened and was, as they'd so hoped it would be, a critical success. Frances, pale-eyed – exhausted – intense, tugged at the heart strings, really came up trumps. The general consensus was that this new Hamilton play under the direction of the bright new Roddy Pincent was 'hard-nosed', was 'interesting'. *Time Out* lauded it, labelled it forever 'The flip side of M.A.S.H'.

Generous to a fault Desmond sent his cuttings across to Ballyross, slips of paper placed on one side now in the dining room as Boyle, in the kitchen, concentrated on an altogether different piece of print. The boy, Sean Maguire, had been arrested. 'Cowboys,' said Dada as he passed it across to his son. Boyle studied it, a column of print, black marks on white paper: 'In connection with the murder of Mr Crawford Ferguson, Rossbawn, Mr Sean Maguire (17) . . .'

Aimee appeared for breakfast, pin smart, chirping, Boyle attempted to roll a cigarette, Dada, triumphant leant against the range, no shirt, a ragged pair of trousers hoisted with a belt, his thick dark hair still wet. Boyle fished matches from his pocket and lit his cigarette, studied the newspaper, he must have been a fool . . .

'You're very intrepid,' commented Aimee on Dada's early morning swim.

'Ah,' he said, 'Yes,' and took himself off and out again.

Aimee poured a tiny portion of Special K into her bowl, 'What are you doing today Boyle?'

'Is Jack about?' he asked.

'He's about somewhere, I don't think he's feeling very well. Do you have to smoke that at breakfast?'

'Excuse me,' he picked up the paper and left the room.

'Boyle! Hang on a minute.'

'Yes?'

'Does this Mrs Devlin come today?'

'Mrs Devlin, she does.'

Not the most sociable family thought Aimee left alone and what's more they'd left the washing up. However Mrs Devlin would appear presumably, that would give her something, someone to get her teeth into.

Boyle let himself into the dining room and firmly closed the door. He felt now as though he were being hollowed out, scooped dry, black marks on white paper but he couldn't read it, something sucked relentlessly at all the softness inside him, took it away and left him gaping. So Sean had been picked up, by Mark perhaps or someone like him, a man doing his job grateful for a modicum of success. A suspect, the papers said, these days they hung onto suspects, a good long time.

Boyle typed the name, Sean Maguire in his daily record beneath the name of Ferguson, Rossbawn. Neighbours.

Boyle gazed through the window at the garden, hardly recognising it in the sun. Did he love this country, did he love this place . . . He bit at his nails as he sat before the typewriter.

Neighbours.

There was intimacy in these killings, a fearful thing, a dreadful audacity. Terror. A daily reckoning, like this daily list, going down like ninepins so they were. Sudden death, quick, never unexpected. His list filled pages, pages, and while he'd been writing it, shall we say religiously, its violence, the violence of Northern Ireland, had eroded more than anyone seemed prepared to acknowledge, to admit. People, he'd been around these people for forty years, and most of them had never seen a corpse unless dressed, done-up properly in an open coffin. Now bodies were strewn about the place, a stage just littered with corpses. Bodies, bodies shoved into black plastic body bags and policemen, boys themselves, out in the muck with shovels, bits and pieces, arms and legs, unidentified, ringless hands. And yet, what was it that witnesses remembered? For Boyle it was the woman's handbag lying hopeless, open on the pavement after the ambulance had gone. The pension book and the photographs of the grandchildren, the spilt compact and not the blood. Regularity, similarity took the dignity from death and robbed it of its ritual. One remembered, suffered from, the aftermath, detritus, superficial mess. Like history itself, one small piece of tesserae that made up the grand mosaic, Boyle thought of Sean's walk as he sat in the dining room, Sean's walk, a loping gait, enthusiastic, eager, foolish, and whatever happened to him now, convicted of conspiracy or perhaps eventually set free, that walk would not be quite the same again. Boyle raised his head as he felt someone looking through the window, Dada, waiting for him to help him move some cattle. His face flushed pink, feeling himself discovered, but he nodded, rose, went out. Neither of them spoke.

Jack was ill. He lay pink-faced and sweating in Boyle's bedroom too miserable to complain. He slept out the days in a fever refusing every offer of food, even an ice-cream and a frozen lolly called 'Zoom' were rejected. Dada was concerned about his grandson but not worried, insisting that a period of prostration was quite common to English visitors to Ireland on account of the softness of the air and that this same softness was quite liable to set even an adult back before it set him up.

The child lay for several days, his temperature just above the mark. After his mother had left the room, quit the playing with his hair which she thought soothing but irritated him, he lay like a feather in his uncle's bed and watched the wallpaper go up and down. With effort he tried to decipher the pattern, he followed it with his watery eyes, he knew the rhythm was upset but could not perceive, God love him, that it was merely one piece hung upside down. In the July heat beyond the windows conversations seemed to hang in the air long after the talkers had passed; hung like wedges of cold pudding, unexplained and out of context. He wanted his daddy but was offered toys, felt pens and chocolate buttons. Doors opened and shut, people passed down the corridors, windows opened. He heard his mother laugh. The telephone rang and was or wasn't answered. He longed alternately for a drink or the lavatory which was cold and shivery and a long way down the corridor. Night swam with day and morning merged peacefully into afternoon. Aimee insisted on a doctor who was very pleasant and reassured her at length as he found her rather attractive. He looked into the child's ears with a torch and down his throat but tonsils were not inflamed. It was just a fever, he said, the heat, and probably as Dada had diagnosed, merely a reaction. The 'wee cub' was tired and had a sort of flu although he didn't specify which sort.

Boyle hovered in the background quite convinced the child was going to die. He sat by him in the old familiar room and talked to the little pink face about what fun they might have together once he had recovered and by doing this found that he was recovering himself. Gradually the wallpaper settled down and when Boyle called into the bedroom Jack stopped looking beyond him to see his mother. For Aimee was dutiful rather than imaginative, if the child was ill it was peace and quiet that would get him better; grateful to have a little time to herself she let him lie, quite happy to let Boyle interfere. Boyle bathed the face and the little squidgy hands and on the question of rejected 'Zooms' recited by memory the poem 'Bad Augustus'.

Boyle's seesaw stilled and flattened out, momentarily balance returned

Free, Aimee explored the garden, got to know the house. She thought not that this place was different from London or different from their own cottage but that it was, undoubtedly different altogether. Something about the house and what she had so far glimpsed of a neighbouring countryside lent a sense of difference that disorientated her, that she really didn't like. Keen to put her finger on the problem she felt it was actually the house, the grounds, that unsettled her the most. To be surrounded, as she was now, by an all pervasive air of gradual deterioration confused her and only sharpened her sense of what she felt to be right and proper. Her eye could find no peace inside or outside the house, something would have to be done. And it would have been done, in England it would have been done. Aimee knew about old houses, had grown up in one herself. Old houses were a privilege and the constant repair and maintenance to them the price one paid. A house like this, the grounds, were a responsibility, ignore them and one found, sooner than one expected, one had a millstone round one's neck. Looking at Ballyross and wandering through its gardens, treading carefully across the broken paving, picking up baling twine here, noticing a fertiliser bag blown into a corner, a line of breeze blocks half supporting a crumbling wall, she raged at the occupants who had allowed things to go this far. Someone had made an abortive attempt to clear one tiny flower bed but this apart, anarchy, the word she had been searching for, anarchy reigned supreme. It was all quite frightening. She pointed out one chimney to Dada saying that it looked really quite dangerous as it was, but he seemed unconcerned, disinterested. Saying that now wasn't the time to be lighting fires and that he'd get a boy to see about it later. Don't put off till tomorrow what can be done today was Aimee's maxim, that's why she'd insisted on getting the local doctor, one couldn't take any chances with a child.

Dada was disorganised if not simply lazy; Boyle was blinkered and preoccupied. Even she could see that the building required substantial re-pointing at the very least. The house she supposed, was Georgian, but the original shape had been most horribly obscured by bits and pieces stuck on apparently at random with no feeling for line, for architecture at all. No one mowed the lawn. No vegetable patch, no greenhouses, nothing. Farmers were notoriously disinterested in gardens but they could have done something, surely? They could have grown tomatoes outside easily in this heat. She read in the papers that people in England were growing green peppers in their flower beds, really they might have made some effort.

The house opened onto a broken terrace from which sunken, perilous steps led down to a large mossy lawn partly shadowed by an enormous Wellingtonia which took the light from most of the upstairs windows, and at the bottom of the lawn was a veritable forest of purple rhododendrons, quite wild, quite out of all control.

Following Dada's trodden path she had found the lake, brightest blue in the sunshine, sculpted from fields which sank down into it and dotted over with islands, patches of green, some wooded, some divided into tiny fields where animals grazed quite incongruously anchored in the deep water: for looking at it she knew instinctively that it was deep. Down here there was a lean-to boat house and, a little to one side, a jetty, a wooden planked affair cushioned with tractor tyres. It really was a shame she thought that they didn't use the boat, no point surely living in such a beautiful spot if one didn't take advantage of the facilities. She'd have to see what she could do. She breathed in the soft air, feeling purposeful. Boating would be fun, lovely for Jack when he was better.

As she stood a helicopter scattered the sky and she waved happily at it. It was, she felt, now, her image of lake and not the garden, like looking at a series of travel posters.

37

'Ireland – you'll love it!'

Small figures moving silently in tiny fields, haystacks, dusty dumplings straight from sepia prints of a world gone by, moved on by the rush. Far out cruisers moved at a leisurely pace, the noise of their engines coming back to her after the sudden deafening of the helicopter. Ducks swam, birds sang, perfect peace.

She looked again at the lake, it was beautiful. Fine for an adult but perhaps a little dangerous for a child? Deep, lapping water . . . could they fence this part of the garden, would they do it? It was dangerous like this, coming so suddenly onto the lough shore, she'd ask about a fence, dreadful if anything happened to Jack and children were such terrors at breaking loose, at getting out. The garden at the cottage had been quite safe, she'd even tied up the gate, you couldn't be too careful. She would have a word with Dada, with Boyle, he was the one more easy to manipulate. Yes she felt strong and energetic too.

Walking back through the lough shore field preparing her case she cast her glance down the drive and to the gates. First impressions were awfully important and all those weeds around the gates, the milk crate and the abandoned tins were frightful. Boyle should get down there with a scythe, he really should. She turned her gaze from the gates with a feeling of distaste, a good wooden five barred gate with a cattle grid would have been more suitable. Dada wouldn't go on forever and it was her job to see that by the time they eventually did inherit the place was saleable at least.

Eager to tackle things she popped in on Jack who was dozing, put a scarf around her head, rolled up her sleeves and set to to Brasso the door knocker. Her face was brown in the sunshine, full of youth and life and it was thus that Mark first saw her.

Desmond missed Aimee, whilst trying to force his brand new sweater into Bernie's drawer. It was a mistake this sweater, forty quid, an impulse buy and a bad one. Ivan's fault of course, Desmond sat back on his heels and cursed Ivan, cursed himself for being so wrongly influenced by him. Ivan was an old mate, another one, their paths hadn't crossed for several years but he'd turned up out of the blue, and with a wife to boot, at the play and taken Desmond out for dinner. Ivan was as smooth as Desmond was rough, they ate at Wheeler's, Dover Sole, charged to the BBC no doubt.

He'd known Ivan way back, Ivan's father was a novelist, Ivan wanted to write books too, Desmond was trying to write plays, they met at this stage at this time. Ivan had not been successful but he was anything but a fool, he joined the BBC. First as an Arts producer with radio, then to television, working his way up all the time through general programmes until now, to hear him at dinner, he had the place sewn up. So they'd met when they'd both been struggling and neither were struggling now.

Ivan was ambitious and he kept his fingers clean. In the intervening years since they had met, Desmond had rather enjoyed despising him, denouncing him as a careerist who had crept into the BBC on his father's back, keeping a close eye on Ivan's cautious triumphs, boring Aimee down to the cotton socks about this other man, reassuring himself in the process that he had made the right decision, kept to the chosen moral path, writing or be damned. In Desmond's book Ivan had become distilled as 'middle of the road', he had forgotten how smooth he really was, how utterly persuasive. The jumper was proof of this. For Ivan always had a motive and he always disguised it well. He did not take anyone, old friend or otherwise out to dinner without a reason, a distinct purpose in mind. The purpose had been Ireland.

Desmond abandoned the drawer, the bedroom, and walked out and up by Colville Gardens to watch the ragged children swing; in the flat he felt ridiculously paranoic. He sat on a swing himself and the kids eyed him with animal curiosity, he felt delicate, he hoped they would not throw stones.

Ivan wanted Desmond to do something on Ireland, a joint, middle-of-the road event. He had conceived a series temporarily labelled *Counterpoint*. Ireland was designated one of the subjects of this series and his researchers, trying to find something nice to say, had come up with the Hamilton articles, actually written by Boyle, on the ancient tradition of stone carving in Fermanagh: 'Enduring archaism of stone carving in the area may be explained to some extent by the Geographical isolation of the county. Absence of Norman settlement certainly played its part in the conservation apparent in the Medieval period. Traditions persist associated with the Pagan religion. Archaistic tendency among the Lough Erne stone carvers often leads to difficulties in dating their work accurately . . .' All good stuff, and his idea had been to build a forty minute film loosely around these carved heads and standing stones, spicing it up a bit with Pagan practices and the general air of Celtic twilight and Yeats's voice raised here above a whisper. The Celtic inheritance, the Celtic connection, counterpoint to bombs in prams and running teenage riots.

The articles were Boyle's work, whether Ivan assumed Desmond had written them or that Desmond would assume responsibility for them in any case, was not made clear. Desmond hardly knew what Ivan was on about but this fact was glossed over too, for Desmond was a name now, and a name was a handy peg to hang it on. He'd flattered Desmond, he'd done it very well. There would be room in this film for the playwright to talk about his roots, his inspiration, his mentors, another angle on writers and places and Desmond had fallen for it, the fool. Hadn't he been out that very morning and bought that Aran sweater, forty quid's worth of itchy wool that made him look like a fat, fish-finger fisherman, a pint drinker, a middle-aged exile going to seed, a big, white slug. Yes, Ivan had given him ideas. The sweater had been a symbol, far more symbolic that he looked awful in it and he couldn't even fit it into a drawer, couldn't fit it in without taking out the rest of his stuff, his T-shirts and jeans. Very symbolic that.

Forty quid down the drain and the point is, Desmond said to himself legs dangling on the little swing, the thing is that the money would be good. And he couldn't say 'no' to publicity, could he? Difficult really. The sweater had been a disappointment but he was getting over that. Wandering back to the flat, calmed, recovered, he heard the sound of his own voice, a bit more broguey than usual. He saw himself, he couldn't resist it, he saw himself in the Aran sweater shot from his good side and looking thin, he saw himself, a blackthorn stick in his hand, perhaps a dog, walking in a light Irish mist, perhaps even a drizzle. Standing by the stone that he and Boyle used long ago to play around but here he was a different man, Hamilton flanked by Synge, by O'Casey, by Yeats. A man and his dog, a playwright and his past. It was far too hot for the sweater of course but he might find a use for it in the evenings. Each race on Portobello identified itself by its hair, its clothes, its badges. Desmond was an Irishman, he might wear the sweater draped across his shoulders, casually . . .

Rather than telephone his brother, he wrote to Boyle, a guarded letter saying that he might be over in the summer, that he was reviving his interest in old stones and would be grateful if Boyle could send him over some stuff to whet his appetite somewhat. Re his visit nothing was fixed or arranged, it was only, he repeated, in the early stages of development, only an idea.

Boyle carried the tea tray across the garden, down from the house to where Mark and Aimee sat in the shade of the Wellingtonia. Jack, proudly in step with him, carried the sugar. The garden was humpy, uneven and he carried the little pot near to his chest, very careful not to spill, not to upset. Mummy was very busy these days and more keen than ever on peace and quiet. Even when she was lying on the chair sunbathing she called it 'busy'. It interested Jack, his mother in the sun and he asked her why her titties went flat and sort of sideways when she lay down. When the men were about she covered herself with a T-shirt, you could still see them but they took on another shape. This was interesting for a little boy but she was really rather boring. These days she lay about quite a bit, except of course when Mark was there when she leant forward to catch his every word, her eyes eager, working like a bird, watching. She'd said, 'Call him Uncle Mark darling, like Uncle Boyle,' but he had flatly refused. One of anything would do.

Boyle proceeded with the tray, watched Mark watching him approaching. 'Hello again.'

'Hello.'

He placed the tray beside Aimee, sat down a little way from the rug. He opened his book but didn't read it, covertly he looked hard at the rug. The rug. During these past weeks, things he hadn't seen for ages, people he had not expected to meet again . . . changes in the house, things recovered from his childhood from the past . . . This rug was another one of these things. Its plaid pattern, lying on the grass, dappled by the shade. He used to knot the tassels of this rug. There! He could see a bit that he had sucked and chewed.

Aimee poured, tea first etc, just like that first afternoon. There were biscuits too on the plate; not chocolate ones because 'no one wanted chocolate in this heat'. Jack would have liked chocolate but he got 'Nice' biscuits and 'Petit Beurre'.

'Boyle,' Aimee handed him his tea, 'I was just saying to Mark that badminton would be fun.'

'Badminton Bear,' said Jack.

'Paddington,' corrected Aimee automatically. 'Badminton is a game.'

'Twit,' said Mark patting Jack on the head as he leaned forward to accept his tea before taking up his former, languid position on the rug. Now Boyle watched Mark, no guns in the garden since that first day, but Mark now a familiar figure. This watching was a little game too, points for pretending not to do it, for pretending not to notice it was being done. He wore today an open-necked shirt, casual slacks. Casual? Was he casual, was he really relaxed? Boyle doubted it, like the red cat sleeping on the windowsill one knew he was really still on duty, still alert.

'I used to play.'

'It could be fun.'

'Just a knock about.'

You could get a net for under a fiver, Mark could bring some rackets from the camp. Everyone could muck in – Boyle was everyone – yes everyone could because it was just a game really, not a sport. Well it was a sort of sport.

'Let's do it,' said Aimee. They'd get it organised, no point putting off today what tomorrow . . .

Boyle went up on the seesaw thinking of today and yesterday, tomorrow, examining the rug which lay curled within his grasp, wondering. Jack just ate the biscuits, a pragmatist at heart he concentrated on his tea.

'No. Boyle's being really boring about the boat,' Aimee was saying. She used the word boring a lot, it meant difficult. Boyle ignored her. 'Aren't you Boyle? It's so silly, I mean how do you know it's no good unless we have proper look. At least you could get it out of the water.' Boyle kept quiet, Mark was such a fool he would probably volunteer to swim beneath it with a torch.

'Quite a job to get it up don't you think?'

'No.'

'What's the problem then?'

'Even if the bottom's okay, which I doubt, it would be too heavy for you Aimee.'

'Surely I can decide that.'

Silence.

'We could have a look at it for her, couldn't we?' suggested Mark, amiable, gentlemanly. 'Not really fair to write it off.'

Silence.

Their eyes met. 'More tea.'

'Thanks. This is heaven you know.'

'Bit gnatty.'

'I'm only sorry we had to meet in such unfortunate circumstances,' he addressed this to Boyle.

'Why unfortunate?' asked Aimee.

'Oh, nothing really. I came up here after a spot of local trouble. No idea of course that this was where Desmond hailed from.'

'Small world,' she smiled at him, 'have another biscuit, do. What was the local trouble,' she went on, 'something awful?'

Boyle felt rather sick, he studied the rug.

'Yes. One of your in-laws' neighbours I'm afraid, shot.'

'What dead?'

'Mmm.'

Mark looked embarrassed.

'That's dreadful.'

'There's a lot of it about,' said Boyle unable to keep the peevishness from his voice.

'That doesn't make it any better. Ugh,' she shivered, 'bit close to home. Did you get anyone?'

Boyle's heart thumped. 'I don't think we ought to talk like this in front of Jack really,' he said.

'He doesn't understand.'

'I do!'

'I suppose you're right. It's horrid to think about, especially on a lovely day. It's gorgeous here don't you think,' she said turning to Mark.

'Fantastic,' he agreed awarding it a tick.

'Gnats Mummy!' said Jack.

Has he been charged? Boyle wanted to ask, What's happening? How long will he be held. Where is he, how long?

'I am getting gnats Mummy.'

'In a minute, darling. Hang on. Let Mummy talk.'

'I'm all itchy.'

'Hot summers always remind one of childhood,' said Mark ignoring the protestations of the present child. 'Looking back the weather was always baking.'

'We used to go to Sussex,' she said. 'Every year. It sounds boring really, we thought it was wonderful. Do you know Sussex?'

Boyle looked at Jack who was itching and then down at the rug, at the grass. A small creature moved in it. Mark put his tea cup down on an ant, covered it in darkness for a moment, it emerged, unscathed, went on.

'Mummy!'

'I'd better get Jack to bed. Ooh!' she said, 'my foot's gone to sleep.' Mark offered his hand. 'Now remember,' she said to Boyle, 'you and Mark go and have a look at the boat, you promised.'

He did not remember promising.

'I don't think this lady's going to give you any peace until you do,' said Mark.

They walked up the garden together, Mark with the tray. Flying ants swarmed from corners of the broken paving. It was hot, hot, hot. Together the men hauled the boat out of the water and up to the hard standing of the boat house.

I think it's okay. It is heavy I agree, Mark talked to himself. Needs a coat of paint. You could anti-foul it? Not worth it really I suppose. I'd just rub it down, paint it.

But he wasn't going to be doing all that. Boyle wanted to protest that there was a farm to run but what was left of their farm didn't take much running.

'How long's it been in the water? Since the beginning of the season?'

'A good time.'

'I thought you lot all had webbed feet down here. It's a shame not to take advantage don't you think. Quite a good tourist trade down here, everything considered.

'Yes, I believe there is.'

The man had a placatory tone, Boyle liked him less and less.

Now he ran his hand across the bow. It would be nice he thought to get Aimee out in this boat, off dry land.

'These clinker built jobs go on forever don't they. Is it a local boat, has it got a name?'

'A cot.'

'Cot.'

Boyle could have told him about this boat building,

about the large cots that carried the cattle across to the islands but he wouldn't give this man the satisfaction.

'Marvellous how these trades go on, year after year. I always think . . .'

Together they walked along the shore, the gnats hovering. 'I wanted to ask you?' Boyle said.

'Ask away.'

'What happened to Maguire? I read that he was picked up.'

'Which Maguire? Out here?'

'Yes, after Ferguson . . . There was some connection presumably?'

'Oh I think so. I think so.'

'Did you pick him up?'

'No, I didn't actually. RUC.'

'I suppose he's in Belfast?'

Mark shrugged.

'What'll happen?'

'Not a great deal. They won't prove it.'

'You don't think it was him then?'

'God knows.'

'Then what are they holding him on?'

'Conspiracy probably. They're all at it. Small fish I shouldn't wonder. Nevertheless he got his fingers burned,' he said confusing his metaphors. 'It's a nasty business you know,' he said confident, confidential.

Boyle stopped for a moment thinking, wondering how much he could ask, how far he could go. 'Is that how you see it? Is that how you feel? If you don't mind me asking.'

'Sorry?'

'You said it was a business, a nasty business.'

'Well,' Mark shrugged, it was one of his mannerisms. When challenged he shrugged. 'Call it what you like old chap, it's hardly very pretty.'

No. Ferguson must have fallen slap onto the concrete parlour floor, blood in the filth like at a calving.

Boyle took a last look at the view across the water,

before turning with the image of its familiar beauty still in him, away from it and up and back through into the garden.

'You never thought of getting the hell out? Going to England like Desmond?'

'No.'

'Pity,' said Mark tactlessly. 'Home is where the heart is I suppose?'

Boyle did not reply, and the growing silence between them became strained.

'I'll have to be making tracks I think,' said Mark now in a louder voice. 'You may tell Aimee that I, personally, will row her out on the lake.'

'I'll give her a shout if you like.'

That moment Aimee's head appeared out of one of the upstairs windows. 'What's the verdict?'

Mark pronounced the boat fit.

'Great,' she said, 'marvellous.' She beamed good humour and sunshine from above.

'When?'

'Mummy!' came a disembodied voice. 'Mummy!'

'Just pop in. There's always someone here, or give me a ring. Whatever. Desmond's given me strict instructions to stay put,' she pulled a face.

'I should think so too.'

'Mumeeeeeeee!'

'I'll have to go. Don't forget.'

'I won't.'

'I'm sorry I missed your father again,' said Mark, heading for his car.

'He's a hard one to catch.'

'I'd like to meet him.'

'We must arrange something.'

'Well. Good to see you,' he put out his hand presumably for another damn good shake. 'Sometime in the week then.' But still he lingered by the car. 'Jack's a fine little chap isn't he?' he said starting the engine at last, 'a super little specimen.'

'Yes.'

'Well marching orders, be seeing you. Don't say it. I'll do the gate.'

Boyle could not bring himself to smile. 'If you would,' he said, 'if you would.'

Boyle felt very peculiar, decisive but peculiar. No point crying over spilt milk, he thought, steady the jug. He lit a cigarette, the first that afternoon; he didn't smoke in front of Mark, almost as if the soldier might interpret it as a sign of weakness. Over the last few weeks the details he had forgotten about Mark, the school boy, had been gradually drawn in by what he saw now of Mark, the man; more than his shoes were polished. So. Work to do, work to do. Boyle went round to the old sheds where he had earlier rediscovered his mother's trowels, forks and secateurs. Taking the axe he put it under his arm and walked smartly down across the proposed badminton court, back down to the boat house. Jack would be having little sandwiches with Aimee in the kitchen, pink and clean after his bath, the chalky smell of baby powder white between his toes.

He swung at the hull of the boat with the axe but succeeded only in chipping the rim. It took a strong arm to swing an axe and he put down his cigarette and swung again, holding the axe with both hands, putting his body behind each blow. It was more difficult than he'd expected, a difficult angle against the grain of the wood, but he did it. A hole in the side that's what he was after. As he struck at it once more the past came back, as slithers of paint, each representing a different summer; black and green, marine blue, covered the ground. He swung and swung almost disjointing his shoulder, quite exhilarated. There! There! There! A good hole, that would fox them! He stood back and looked; quite a substantial hole. No boat today or tomorrow, boating was off! He left the lake and gathered up the rug in his arms as he went back up the garden, smelling his mother in the plaid. It was hard to know what to do with the proposed badminton court. At the moment he felt quite strong enough to undermine it with a tunnel, to dig a massive hole and sneakily replace the sods over the top . . .

Like a moth to a flame he sought Aimee out in the kitchen. There were some leftover sandwiches on a plate, he took one.

'Greedy,' she said looking at him as if she was his mother but offering him the plate. 'Go on, have them. Honestly, we've only just had tea.' But she smiled, 'I suppose you're parched as well,' she said in poor imitation of his accent, 'I'll make another pot.'

Jack made car noises with his sandwich and raced it round his plate. 'Rum, brum, brum, brrummm.'

'He's not hungry,' said Aimee filling the kettle the proper way, possible now with the empty sink. 'Too hot isn't it darling?'

Although it was nearly seven pm, sun still streamed in through the kitchen windows.

'Go on,' said Aimee patting Jack on the head, 'But quietly, please.'

Jack wandered off leaving his sandwich stalled on the table. 'I just collapse at this time of the day,' said his mother throwing herself into a chair to wait for the kettle.

'The heat,' said Boyle. 'Tea's good, it really quenches,' he continued absently. Relief flooded through him as he sat there, total relief.

'You've worked up quite a sweat anyway,' said Aimee.

'Have I?' Boyle removed his glasses and felt his forehead beneath his hair. 'I think you work very hard Aimee,' he said quickly, 'You really do work hard.'

'Mrs Devlin works hard,' corrected Aimee on one of her favourite topics. 'These people need to be told what to do, you have to put a cloth in their hands and point them in the right direction . . .'

The kitchen was bright, the curtains washed, the table clean, the draining board held only Jack's sandwich plate, the bread board and some knives, the remains of one small meal rather than a whole day's dishes. The floor had been darkened with polish, the dresser cleared, the newspapers folded by the wireless no longer slipped between the arm and seat of his father's chair. Only the red cat considered himself beyond the jurisdiction of Aimee's law; a box with a blanket in it had been set for him beside the range, he walked round and sniffed but had adamantly refused to succumb. Although forced to evacuate the fruit bowl he continued to sleep across the windowsill tipping the vases of flowers that Aimee took a long time to arrange.

Boyle was conscious of his sweat and touched at his forehead, his hand shook. His back was soaking and his chest, his upper lip wet, sweaty. But it was good to be out of the heat, to drink tea in this bright room. Aimee looked well, her face, her bare arms, her neck and shoulders, brown, her cheeks with a high fresh colour from being out all day. Jack in his pyjamas, pale blue with 'bed time' embroidered on the front, was skidding up and down the corridor, 'being quiet', in a pair of Dada's wellington boots that came right up to his thighs. Children change all the time, thought Boyle listening, remembering Jack ill, the flushed face, the damp blonde hair. I love him, I love him, he thought. I love Jack. Jack looked so like Desmond, so like Desmond.

Aimee was reading a magazine: 'After-sun milk for a longer lasting tan . . .'

'Thank you for all this,' said Boyle almost to himself. 'The woman's touch,' he explained, 'Very nice.'

'Thank you, Boyle.'

'Do you have any word from Desmond?'

'No.' She shrugged her shoulders as Mark had done, perhaps it was an English thing this shrugging.

'But he is still coming.'

'Apparently. When of course is another matter.'

'I expect you miss him,' dared Boyle.

Aimee smiled at the intimacy. Boyle was a funny old stick, 'Well, no. Do you know at the moment I must admit that really I don't! It's rather nice to have a bit of time off, you know.'

'Oh yes, I know.' Boyle nodded vigorously. She was so pretty, when she was being nice and the sweating had stopped. She was being intimate with him now, for the first time, almost as if she knew what he'd done to the boat, action not impotence and he'd just done it. Thought about doing it and done it, bloody done it! She was talking to him now as an equal, not perhaps as she would to another man but rather as a special friend, a confidante, a member of the family to whom things could be said, someone who understood the lie of the land and didn't need to be explained to.

'I suppose he'll turn up when his play's finished,' he said.

'Mmm,' said Aimee reading again.

'I wouldn't like to be in London in this heat!'

'Nor me,' said Aimee rubbing her hand over her shoulder blade. 'I've been bitten,' she said, 'under that wretched tree. Look!' she turned her head and examined her shoulder, felt a large lump.

Boyle leant across the table. 'It's the lake,' he said, 'always gnats. That's a cleg.'

'A what?'

'A cleg.' Boyle made a buzzing noise worthy of Jack, incongruous in this timid, wary man. They laughed. Boyle looked at her shoulder, rubbed red, Aimee felt him looking and stood up.

'Well. Time for me to get Sunny Jim to bed,' she said.

'I have enjoyed our talk.'

'So have I, Boyle. Your father's not around much is he?'

Boyle shook his head, the sweating had started again.

'What does he get up to?' she asked standing in the doorway.

'This and that,' Boyle wasn't being evasive. He really didn't know how his father spent his time. 'Driving about, chatting, buying a bit here, selling a bit there, friends.'

'The right touch. Like Desmond,' said Aimee.

'That's it. Will I do the tea things for you?'

'Thank you,' she smiled and went out, calling for her son.

Aimee carried the child upstairs stooping to pick up a day's toys on the way. She helped him brush his teeth and automatically gritted her own, looked at her brown face in the mirror.

'You know what Mummy,' said Jack as she tucked him

up, 'the lake's on fire!'

'Mmm,' she kissed him.

'Honestly Mummy, I saw it.'

'Well you can't see it from this window. There, there's teddy, now snuggle down, go to sleep.'

'Will someone come and put it out?'

'It's the sunset, sweetie, the sun's going to bed and so are you. Now, sleep.'

'But it's really burning Mummy, you can hear it.'

'Good night,' she said firmly. 'Sleep tight and don't let the clegs bite.'

'Mummy, Mummy! What are clegs?'

'Never you mind,' she said, 'I'll tell you in the morning.'

Closing the door – for she'd never had any fuss with him about night-lights or open doors – she walked back along the corridor to her own room, put on a dab of scent, patted at her hair, she'd like to get it cut but didn't know whether she dared let anyone touch it here; it would do another week or so. She took a cardigan for later; it was still hot, sunset or not. Boyle's nursery room door was open. Neither he or his father ever closed a door or a window and the corridor she noticed was really awfully bare, could really do with some carpet, an old runner on the floor would brighten it, pictures on the wall, something. But all these tasks were pleasant to her because she was happy although she had not yet admitted to herself just why this was so. As she put her hand on the nursery door knob making a mental note to get Mrs Devlin up here with her cloth, she glanced out through the barred windows which looked down the garden to the lake.

'Boyle,' she yelled, 'Boyle!'

She went back to the door and then back again to the window. He was in the kitchen, he'd have that wretched wireless on, he wouldn't hear her.

'Boyle!' She dashed down the stairs.

'What is it?' he said. He had a drying up cloth in his hands, a cup.

'It's on fire!' she screamed, 'It's on fire!'

He dropped the cup.

'The lake, the garden!'

They ran together to the front door, Jack appeared at the head of the stairs, 'Mummy!'

'Go to bed!' she screamed.

She and Boyle ran down the uneven garden but could only get within twenty yards of the line of rhododendrons which gave out a mass of smoke.

'Oh God!' said Boyle.

Aimee wrung her hands. 'Do something,' she said, 'Quickly.' He looked at her. 'Call the fire brigade you idiot!' But still he stood, stunned. '999 come on, quickly!'

Jack was in the garden now and she scooped him up as she ran, the cardigan over her shoulders dropped onto the grass.

He was absolutely useless! She had to dial the number. Fire, she thought, Oh God fire! as she gave the name and the address. Fires in this weather! Picnickers with lighted matches marched through her imagination. 'Oh God, fire!' she thought as she stood by the telephone after passing on the information. Where the hell was Dada? The whole house would go up! She squeezed the child in her arms, fire! fire!

Boyle was incapable of action, frozen in a moment of surprise and shock. Down there in the garden he saw individual leaves, green and glossy, roll up against the heat, coil and wind as if drawn around a pencil, catch fire, grow brittle, flake to nothing! He stood and watched the fire race among the rhododendrons, transfixed.

'Where the hell's your father?' she said grabbing his arm roughly with her free, white hand. 'Where is he?'

'How can I?' said Boyle, 'I can't get to the water, the lake . . .'

'By the field!' she said taking him up the garden. They stood now on the gravel by the flower bed but neither of them moved. It was obviously stupid. What could you do with two buckets in a lake?

'Oh God, Oh God,' moaned Boyle. The fire had really

taken hold, they watched it do so, Aimee's ears primed for the sound of the engines. Boyle listening to the fire, the crackle and spurt, the burning fed by the warm evening air, the lake they couldn't see at that level, hissed and spat, as they turned at last to run down the drive, over the fence and into the lough field.

'It's all your bloody fault,' she said forgetting about Jack. 'Letting them grow up like that. It's a fire risk all that stuff so near the garden!' Boyle followed her as she went downhill to the shore, 'Don't follow me! Get the fence out you idiot! For the fire engine; it'll have to come down here. When's it coming, when's it coming,' she repeated to herself, Jack in her arms at least safe, holding his toy tractor.

'The cattle,' said Boyle, 'What about the cattle?'

'Bugger the cattle! Get the fence out, open the gates!'

Boyle tugged at the fence posts, the ground was as hard as sheer rock. He looked back at Aimee, pulled again and felt the snag as the barbed wire caught the soft heel of his hand. He left it then and ran down the drive opening the huge gates. The sound of their bells was on the road.

'When's it coming, when's it coming?' repeated Aimee.

It came, them: two red engines with bells and noises and confusion, the men still putting on their uniforms as they rode, Dada arrived behind them. The cattle ran down to the lake, the smell of smoke, fear in their nostrils. The first engine went straight over the fence taking it like a tank as if it didn't exist, smashing half of the thorn tree as it passed.

'Go over the field!' shouted Dada taking control and pulled four posts straight out of the earth. The cattle were down in the corner of the field. The fire officers, back in the machine, thundered down the sloping field to take the water from the lake. The second engine too went across the field but gave the thorn tree a wide berth. 'You move the cattle out,' one shouted.

Seeing his father, Boyle ran then as he had as a child. Down the field and into the smoke with his arms wide open. 'Shoo! Whoa! Whoa!' getting behind the animals in the thick of it, moving them up the field.

There were other men now coming through the gates. A boy and his father, Billy Ferguson was there. They moved the cattle together, 'Whoa, Whoa!' they yelled and shouted. 'Shooraaah!'

Aimee withdrew, leant against the warm brick of the house. Jack in her arms watched in amazement and terror, unable to cry as a steer ran over his mother's cardigan. Boyle and the men disappeared, herding the cattle willy-nilly across the road and into the neighbouring field. The huge hoses spilled from their reels and sucked the water from the lake, pumping, the noise of the engines stilled, the shouts of the men in uniform wildly at odds with the summer evening.

They all thanked Christ for the earth being dry and hard. It had been quick because they had been able to drive across the field, in a normal year this would not have been possible at all. The chief fire officer present reassured Aimee that there was no danger now and hoped he would be offered tea, but for once Aimee had forgotten her manners. They had it out in an hour. The lake killed it, acres of blue. As to how it happened no one was certain. Just one dropped match was enough in this heat, there'd been a terrible fire at Derrygonnelly, acres of forest lost. It was all over and without tragedy. Despite the excitement it was only Dada who sat up. Sat in the sitting room his armchair turned to face through the long windows. One engine and its men stayed for a bit, just in case it might flare up, kept him company until it too was called away. Dada stayed the course, puffed at his pipe, remained and waited for the cat.

Part Two

By the morning the scene had changed, as dramatically as if one curtain had been rolled up by the management, another let down. The view from the front of the house that Mark had admired lying in the garden, that Boyle had wanted Jack to spend the summer with looking from the nursery windows, was not the same.

Now the garden went down into the lake, a smoking mass of burnt and broken wood that spanned the width of the garden, no more than a foot high, was all that was left of the green-black, purple-flowered majesty of the rhododendrons. The boat house and the boat were gone, the jetty remained, the slug-texture and smell of burnt rubber where the tractor tyres had melted.

The lake was clearly visible from all the downstairs windows at the front of the house, no longer something glimpsed between the foliage, it lay now sucking at the shore, dramatically there. The garden appeared bereft, grotesquely shorn. Now the vista was of water, acres and acres of water, water and islands, nothing in between.

They looked in astonishment in the most cloudless blue of days, looked together and returned to look again, wandered dazed on the gravel trying to get their bearings. Like a pubescent excited by a full length mirror they were drawn, drawn to the view.

Jack went back to bed shortly after breakfast because Aimee felt she needed a rest. Dada and Boyle went to see after the cattle. Aimee dealt with the police. 'No,' she said quite firmly, they had no reason to suppose it was malicious. A member of the family had been down to the boat house that afternoon, perhaps a light from a cigarette? On behalf of them all she would like to express her thanks and praise for the prompt efficiency of the fire brigade. Yes they had been very concerned. No, she would not go so far as to call it a tragedy, after all no one had been hurt. She offered the officer coffee. They were very serious times as she probably realised although she was from England, wasn't she? She noticed then and for the first time, his gun, his belt, his flac jacket. One had to be on one's guard, especially in this weather but she wasn't sure to what he was referring, the drought or the Troubles. 'Fierce times,' he said. He looked like a farmer, anxious for his crops, a worried man. Without the lake they might have lost the house. He hadn't been up to the place for a very long time, must be twelve years, he said. Aimee understood. Felt the implication about the state of the place and swiftly took his point, after all the place was really nothing to do with her.

After he had gone Aimee was drawn back to the front of the house to look, the smell of burning was on her clothes and in her hair, she walked down to the water's edge, picking her way through the stubble of burnt wood. Old cans and bottles were all that was left of the boat house. She felt a bit let down now, no one to talk to, no one to sympathise with her. She went back picking up her ruined cardigan, back to the 'phone to ring Desmond in London but the number that she dialled was for Mark.

'How awful! How ghastly!' they said to each other. Yes. He'd heard that morning. 'A bit of a close shave, how ghastly, how grim!'

'Look,' he said, 'Would you like me to pop up? I'm sure I could get away.'

'Would you Mark? I do feel a bit, well, you know, shaky.'

'Of course you do!'

'God knows how it happened,' she said and saying it thought suddenly that it was Boyle who had done it, out of spite. Boyle.

'I'll come up,' he said.

'I'll make some coffee.'

'Give me . . .', he paused and she imagined his wrist as

he looked at his watch and her heart swam out to him, 'Give me twenty minutes.'

'Thanks,' she replaced the receiver slowly in its socket, she knew, saw, that she had taken the first step.

Billy Ferguson told his mother about the fire but it just glanced off her like everything else. When pressed she said she wasn't at all surprised, things being what they were up there, but that he had been right to help, right to lend a hand. You could see the Ballyross set up from the original farmhouse but not from the bungalow that the Fergusons had built together with the money Crawford had brought back from the States: from the bungalow, through the mesh of nylon curtains, one simply saw the fields and that had seemed enough. The doctor had put Betty on Valium, yellow pills to help her sleep as she still had a family to look after. She kept busy with baking and the floral society. The red hot pokers in the garden had to be watered in this weather; she watered. All day she longed for the bedroom where she would sit and hold his sweater in her arms. She'd done it up in moss stitch for him that winter, he was rough with his clothes and she'd knitted through the back of every stitch to make it firm. A really well knitted, home-made sweater would last a life time; she hadn't known when she knitted it that his would be so short.

Up at Ballyross tension gathered in darkening clouds and threatened quite to eclipse the sun. Jack picked it up like a magnet with pins and was told that he was 'overtired' when he was really reacting quite reasonably to the unpleasantly hostile atmosphere. It was as if, with the stripping of the rhododendrons and the new clear and uninterrupted view of the lake, the veneer of politeness that had made life feasible between the ill-assorted personalities of Dada, Boyle, Aimee and Mark, was beginning to chip up, had been nastily singed by the fire. The state of undeclared war that crossed, and recrossed the province extended now its clammy fingers to the occupants of the lakeside house, the heat making odd and unpredictable behaviour more than a possibility.

Aimee was not be gainsaid by any man and rode over Boyle like a tank in a field of mushrooms. Ostensibly the trouble centred over the – she considered wilful – destruction of the boat, and though she tackled Boyle at length she did not immediately bring him down.

'You did it deliberately,' she said as they stood above the horror of the garden outside the front door with its bright knocker. 'You deliberately set fire to the boat!'

'Aimee, I did not.'

'You did! What's the point? Why bother, why deny it? You set fire to it, on purpose, because you don't want me, us, to have any fun. You jeopardised the security of the whole house, of Jack, everybody, just because of some petty little vengeance . . .'

'I did not . . .'

'Just because you can't bear it if anybody else has any fun. You want to sit up here and vegetate, fine! Ignore all the resources on your doorstep, let the place go to rack and ruin, it's all right with me, but there's no reason to think you can drag me along with you!' Her tone was superior, furiously cold.

'Now you have it all wrong,' said Boyle, 'It isn't true.'

'Oh yes, it is Boyle,' she didn't touch him but would have liked to clasp his arm, tightly, as she did to Jack when she was annoyed with him in public. 'Oh yes it is. I'm not a fool you know. Your pathetic little puritan ethics . . .'

He listened well, infuriating her more by his lack of response.

'Just because of some petty little grudge against Mark. No! Don't shake your head, I can see it a mile off!'

Aimee raged, she fired the argument, gave it momentum because once she had begun she realised that she really felt like quarrelling, a scrap was what she wanted, what she was going to have. Raging against Boyle she raged against herself, against the unpleasant fact that she was actually married to his brother, Desmond who no longer adored her, who'd said he found her dull. The argument snowballed so that she arrived at something both bigger and different to the original as if these grudges had been pent up in her and that the clearing of the garden had also cleared her way: 'It's just because you don't like Mark, isn't it. Because he's English.'

'No,' said Boyle shaking his head, 'No.'

The telephone was ringing but Aimee went on arguing, 'Well all I can say is, that what you did was bloody irresponsible; you're quite mad, you shouldn't be allowed out!'

'I don't go out.'

'Oh answer the 'phone!'

'Hello,' said Boyle, 'Ballyross. Oh, Desmond,' it was Desmond, blessed relief.

'Boyle? Hello, How's tricks?'

'Give it to me!' said Aimee, taking it. 'Hello. Desmond. Yes, do I, well I am! In a ghastly state! We've had a fire here. No, not in the house, in the garden. Not a bonfire! The rhododendrons were all burnt down. It was awful, you've no idea! Honestly I'm quite shattered!'

'How's Jack?'

'Oh, he's fine, well, he isn't really, poor little thing, up half the night. Darling I wish you were here!'

'Actually that's what I rang for. I'm coming tomorrow.'

'Tomorrow?'

'Yes, That's all right isn't it?'

'Yes, absolutely. Fine.'

'Could Dada meet me?'

'I don't know. I'm sure he could. What time?'

'Five-thirty.'

'He's not here at the moment. Someone will be there.'

'Right, well I'll see you tomorrow then,' he said, 'Okay.'

'Fine.'

In some confusion Aimee replaced the receiver, 'Christ!' but collecting herself she returned to Boyle continuing almost where she had left off as if the fact of Desmond's arrival was immaterial which in a way it was.

'Anyway you'll be glad to hear that we've found another

boat!'

'What?'

'We're taking the Maguires' boat. Mark and I've borrowed it.'

'You're joking.'

'I certainly am not.'

'You can't.'

'Why can't I? What's the matter with you?'

'That was the boat, they used that boat for a murder.'

'So?'

'Aimee please . . .'

'Oh shut up! don't come your sensitive bit with me, Boyle. Anyway I've already rung them, Mark suggested it. They don't mind a bit.'

Boyle was speechless, incredulous.

'Well don't look so dumb,' yelled Aimee. 'A boat is a boat, Boyle,' she explained as if talking to a retarded child, 'A boat is a boat is a boat.'

Boyle looked sullen.

'Look,' she said 'I honestly don't care what you think. I don't care what anyone thinks. I don't give a damn for all your petty little religious differences.'

'It's not that!' Boyle was furious now, 'We've just never . . .'

Aimee shook, her voice was scathing. 'Never what? Never rung them up before, never met them socially . . . Neighbours are for helping each other.' She sighed, it was hopeless. 'Nobody behaves like this in England you're so bloody stupid. And stubborn. It's all on your own heads, this,' she said broadly indicating eight hundred years of political unrest in which England apparently had no part. 'If you could just get together over things like, the boat, it wouldn't be like this. It's absolutely pathetic, puerile,' and as he still made no comment she continued, 'We don't expect you to come with us you know.'

'Good.'

'We're going tomorrow, for the day, we're taking a picnic.'

'I see.'

'And I've told Desmond that Dada will pick him up at the airport.'

'What about Jack?'

Aimee had forgotten Jack. 'I thought Jack, it would probably be better, if he stayed here with you.'

Boyle couldn't help smiling, a helicopter passing overhead took away her comments and he walked away from her, left her be.

'Boyle! She yelled at him but the helicopter turned again and swept over the house flattening the grass in the Well Field. These helicopters are bloody annoying, thought Aimee. What were they doing anyway? Were they training or what? Going over all hours of the day and night. Was the air force in Ireland too? She would ask Mark about it, she really knew nothing at all.

Dada observed but did not intervene and Aimee was wrong to think his lack of comment denoted his approval. Playfully, on unimportant matters, household things, she deferred to him, in their different ways neither of them took this subservience seriously; he was an old Irish man with funny ways, his thoughts, his feelings, hopes or disappointments were beyond her orbit, were of no concern to her. But Dada disapproved, vehemently, silently. Not for religious or moral reasons – Fergusons, Maguires, all one to him – he resented the interference, he resented the cars outside the house, the sound of the telephone, Aimee's laughter, Mark stepping confidently from his car, Aimee who changed the station on the wireless and tidied away his newspapers. Like the red cat and the disputed cardboard box, he neatly avoided the ashtrays placed strategically in his path and continued to be late and often absent for meals. Jack did his heart good, to hear him in the morning long before anyone else was up, his mother was simply Desmond's wife, a good-looker but nothing to do with him. What Desmond did, what Boyle did, was their business and he did not want it brought to his doorstep. Let the Maguires kill the Fergusons, he would observe but he would not become involved. Like the lakeside tree he stood bent against the prevailing wind, formed by the elements, but not brought down.

Desmond sat at the Appletree Bar, Heathrow Airport, he felt mentally and physically ill at ease. After a month in London his flesh looked as if it had been bought by a price conscious mother who expected him to grow into it next term; inside the brand new shirt his stomach sagged, his neck hung in folds, he felt wobbly at the knees, rotten. Ivan and his wife would turn up soon and then he would feel better, at the moment he didn't want to be alone.

Boyle had replied to his letter requesting information, what he had sent had worried Desmond a great deal. In front of him now on the table was Boyle's covering letter, this had upset him too. Rather than look at it again Desmond's eyes followed the crowd, the rich and the sleek who swayed to the airport rhythm; he listened to the forever, click, click, click of the Departures Board, the saccharine announcements: 'Will Mr Taylor meeting Mr Godwin from the Channel Islands please come to the British Airways Information Desk on the second floor/ Flight One Zero Two, now boarding at gate number eight . . .' A bunned Asian woman in European shoes softly mopped in the far distance creating a circle of stillness about herself. Desmond concentrated alternately on her and on the letter which lay on the coffee-ringed formica table, a counterpoint for Ivan this, the crazy and the calm.

Dear Desmond,
It is surprising how things turn out, just when I was, well I think you know what this country's like. I was thinking I'd made a mess d'you see but now that the house is full again . . . we haven't made enough effort have we? Families are important, seeing Jack, you don't know, can't imagine, how it's changed things. Luck comes up when you least expect it, isn't that the case and I had stopped expecting anything at all. And the stones,

you're interested in them are you and I, living here, haven't been out to White Island, oh I can't remember when . . . and the Boa stone, well that was our secret really wasn't it, a family thing, I remember going out there with mother, before you were born or even thought of. I've so much to show you here, everything I've been up to since you've been across the water. Do you remember Archie? Worked up here with Dada in the fifties, had his own sheep up near Derrygonnelly only whose sheep they were? Fierce goings on if you remember! He's still got the place up there, his mother's old place I think it is, but he's an old boy now and he had this bicycle repair shop in the town. I was thinking of getting myself one of those seats for the bicycle, those child's seats with the straps and everything for Jack then we can all go out together to the stone when you come over. It would be safe you see, better than the water, I could take him off flying on the bike! And you're coming home, that's great. If you're bringing friends there's room in the house if you want it. Aimee mentioned they're some friends you had in television, this house hasn't known such life for years. I don't mind any of it as long as you are coming. Here's a sample of the stuff to whet your appetite, you'll have to get acclimatized it's been so long. There's one or two things been worrying me, it's not quite what it was here if you get my meaning, but more of that later on. The bloody cat for one, but anyway we'll have plenty of time to talk. Well, I'll get this into the post for you, I'm glad you've come to your senses after all, glad to hear you're really coming home.

Desmond screwed up the letter in his fist, he wasn't coming home. 'London based, Desmond's London based,' Ivan had explained to his superiors as he set the proposed film in motion. Boyle, on purpose or so it appeared, had got the message wrong. Desmond chucked the letter onto a nearby tray where it lay beside a half-eaten Danish pastry and a flat plastic cup of Coke. As the fire had raged at Ballyross the night before so Desmond, unknowing, had put the pile of clippings and notes that Boyle had sent into the fireplace at Notting Hill and set it all alight. He had not asked for, did not want, a duplicate list of the dead and limbless, he didn't want a thesis on the rubber bullet and its use or of the effects of high velocity shots to the head . . . he wasn't interested in the cutting marked 'New surgery first for Royal Victoria Hospital' or a breakdown of hooligan elements in the UDR. He didn't want the two pieces of blotting paper or the curled pressed flowers between them, he didn't want the tourist brochure underscored, re-punctuated by his brother.

'The loughsiders are shy people but if you get talking to them they are apt to tempt you away from your boat, only 60 peoople to the square mile compared with nearly a thousand in England; Lough Erne, the Amazon without mosquitoes!'

All this had to be funny, had surely to be some kind of joke: some incomplete theory of his brother's written in pencil which as far as he could tell made a bizarre comparison of Irish history, ancient and modern: 'I saw a great flock of black birds coming to us from the depths of the ocean. They settled over all of us and fought with the people of Ireland. They brought confusion on us and destroyed us. One of us I thought struck the noblest of the birds a blow and cut off one of its wings. Invasion it was and dark clouds cast a darkness on the sun.'

Did Desmond care that Boyle titled his casualty list 'The Big A. Buckets of Blood', no, he did not, but he couldn't forget it now could he? On receipt of this heavy envelope from his brother Desmond had at first tried to make the contents add up to something, looked for connections. Was this several pieces of different puzzles, was it simply a handful of stuff taken at random from the top of his brother's desk or did it, God forbid, add up to something other, something else?

Waiting for reality, Ivan and his wife, Desmond's thoughts slid away from the present to childhood memories of Ballyross. Doing jigsaws with Boyle on the floor of the nursery while the rain dripped steadily outside, Boyle going all red and quiet when Desmond had forced him to do the sky. Boyle closed his face when Desmond, when anyone, upset him, Boyle at mother's funeral as closed as a poked-at snail. Boyle stuck up the Wellingtonia on a dare, clinging to the tree unable to go up or down, refusing his younger brother's help, clinging there until Dada came, angry, and had to prise him off the branch, literally tug him off, as if he had no confidence in Dada to get him down safely to the ground.

Desmond was not a superstitious man, he did not believe in anything outside the reality that he could touch, hear, feel, smell or see, but he didn't want to go to Ireland now, wouldn't have gone if he hadn't got himself so stupidly involved. Disarmed as much by Boyle's letter and cuttings as by the fact that he had discarded them, destroyed them, Desmond's anticipated pleasures, of seeing Jack, doing the film, getting a break, now took on the form of indulgence he could not perhaps actually afford. Ivan and Clover turned up, drinks, smiles, off to the departure lounge, Desmond thinking of his father now Dada had the right idea, gloriously isolated, enviably remote.

Boyle and Jack watched from the nursery as Mark helped Aimee into the stern of the boat, handed down their swimming things, sun tan oil, sunglasses. Jack balanced on the bottom rung of the barred window wriggling in his uncle's arms as if by doing so he might be in there with them, sitting across a thwart, running a hand in the water, but Boyle held him firm, secure. Mark undid the painter, born to tie and untie the right knots, and they cast off and out onto the blue-brown water.

Boyle witnessed their going with a sense of overwhelming déjà vu. He knew he did not appear in the scene and watched it impotently with a feeling of infinite weariness as the picnic basket – the picnic basket again – and the rug – the rug again, were handed down into the little boat. Mark rowing the first strokes, Aimee looking forward through her sunglasses across the water to the island. Watching there with Jack, Boyle almost saw the curve move inexorably round and knew that whatever the pattern might be it was now well on the way to completion. He didn't shout out or wave or 'Haloo!' because he knew it was impossible to stop them, that he had no right to do so and, that in any case, they wouldn't understand. He could never make them see a process which he barely grasped himself; he only knew that circles have a way of meeting without joins and, like a garment without seams, cannot be unpicked.

But Jack was easily diverted. Mark had brought him a Dinky fire engine and they took this and the tractor and trailer downstairs and out into the garden. Boyle with his packet of Covent Garden White, Jack with his toys.

The soil in the little flower bed was as dry as dust. The part that Boyle had dug those weeks ago only distinguishable because it held slightly fewer weeds than the rest; the soil in his hands felt like thick grains of sand, so dry that the earth made no dirt mark on his fingers. The midday sun poured down upon them both from the sky of highest emulsion blue, Jack with his hands firmly on the fire engine, 'brum, brum, bruuum', blasting a road through the dirt. Boyle fetched the watering can, they found the rose for it but the rubber was perished and split when he pulled it onto the spout. Boyle pulled out the weeds and watered the seed bed, realising as he did so that the process was easier the other way around. Jack, by this time, had the engine actually in the watering can and was re-enacting the night of the fire in inaccurate and imaginative detail: 'I'm the fire chief,' he said, 'rum, rum, brum, brummmmm. Get that fence out! Bugger you, bugger you! and down comes the fence, rumm, rumm, rumm.' Boyle watched the earth greedily absorb the water. It was hot and he wiped his forehead with his sleeve and read the back of the seed packet: 'Sow in boxes in February and March, plant out, two inches apart, in April.' 'Oh.' He sat right back on his heels and looked down the garden but the boat had disappeared, he held the packet rigid in his hands. 'Brum with me, brum with me!' said Jack.

'Not now.'

Jack sighed just like his mother, a long sigh. 'Please,' he said, 'Please!' and climbed onto his uncle's knee leaving the engine to sink down into the watering can. He patted Boyle gently on the chest the way Aimee patted to soothe him when he cried, pat pat, pat pat. 'Please!' he asked again stretching out the word, 'Why can't we? Why can't we plant the seeds?'

Boyle put his arms round the child trying to pluck his heart up and out of it so that the child's touching wouldn't hurt. He shook his head and bit hard at his lips, tried to speak in his normal, non-committal voice. 'Sorry. It's a bit late really,' he shook the seeds up and down in the packet, up and down because he thought ridiculously that he might cry because he thought it was all too late. 'Oh dear. No, you see, I don't think they'd grow now.'

'Why?'

'They have to be planted in April, or even before that.'

'When's April?'

Boyle took off his glasses and polished them unsuccessfully on his hanky, 'I'm afraid April was ages ago little man. Next year we can do it,' he added hopelessly.

'What can we do now, this year?'

Boyle swallowed hard, 'Well . . .'

'Badminton,' suggested Jack now diverting Boyle. 'Badminton,' he liked the word. They had played earlier in the day, Boyle and Aimee against Mark, Jack in everybody's way. As they could not make up a foursome they had agreed a typically 'fair' rule that the player on his own had the advantage of the flat ground, his opponents having to run up hill to hit the shuttlecock. Boyle had never played anything quite so irritating although it had to be admitted that his experience of ball games as a whole was not great. Even if one hit with all one's might the shuttlecock hardly went an inch. Hitting it reminded him of dreaming. However fond he was of the child, to play with him, and it would have to be under the net, was not something he could contemplate.

'Tell me a story then,' said Jack sensing 'no', 'Go for a walk?'

But Boyle couldn't immediately summon the energy, the heat was sapping.

'Your Daddy is coming tonight,' he stalled.

'Will he bring me something?'

'I expect so.' The conversation brought him precious moments just sitting. He felt shattered and old, as if it really didn't matter whether he stayed out there on the gravel for the rest of his life. Mark and Aimee were out in Sean's boat, and the boy was on his knee. When Desmond came of course the child would go to him, it was only natural. Boyle didn't want to think about it and shook the seed packet again, the tiny dry seeds slithered up and down like grains of salt. 'What are you going to tell daddy when you see him, Jack?'

'The fire,' Jack jumped up and fished the engine out of the watering can, 'and the men, rum, rum!'

Boyle pulled himself up and left the seeds, unopened in the bed, 'Do you want a walk then?'

'And a story!'

'We'll have lunch first and then we'll walk.'

'And then we'll have a story,' insisted Jack, 'Won't we?'

'Where's Mummy?' he asked after lunch.

'On the lake.'

'Why can't we go?'

'She's far away by now.'

'When's she coming back?'

'Tonight.'

'Will I be in bed?'

'I expect so.'

'Will Daddy come and see me?'

'I'm sure he will.'

Jack seemed satisfied with this and bounced on his toes like his father. 'Are you a daddy?'

'No.'

'Why?'
'I'm your uncle.'
'Can I go on your back?'
'You may.'

Boyle lifted the boy onto his shoulders and they went down to the gate, Jack leaning forward and holding onto Boyle's hair. Then on, across the road, to the field which held the recently moved cattle. Boyle set the child on the gate and pulled him a blade of grass to chew. Coming to this gate in this way had over the weeks become a 'thing' with them. Boyle had taught Jack how to climb the gate and how to cross his hands over at the top in order to get down the other side: the first time Jack had simply jumped, leapt, straight out and into the blue, he had absolutely no fear.

Boyle thought of Mark and Aimee going out to the island, the island he had so wanted to share with Sean. Oh Christ! The peace and blue of the afternoon shot through for him, a cloth so punctured with holes that a faint breeze might blow it clean apart. All around in the cloudless sky, the buzz from the grass, the softness of the air and the general stillness of the afternoon, came the sense of horror impending, suspended too high, too far up, for him to see accurately and take avoiding action. It fell on him like a wedge making his pace and thoughts deliberate and slow. Jack was fortunate and untouched, small and brown now after the weeks of sunshine, clever at climbing the gate, taking it for granted, confident with his uncle.

'Why are you sad?' he asked.
'I'm not really sad.'
'Did you want to go with Mummy?'
'No,' Boyle laughed.
'They've got a picnic.'
'I know.'
'Why didn't you go?'
'I don't like the water.'
'Why?'
'Because it's wet,' Boyle tickled the child's ear with a piece of grass.

'Really why. Really why?' chanted Jack standing on the rungs of the gate, leaning forward and letting his hands wave free.

'Very clever,' said Boyle.

'Why uncle? Really why?'

'Oh, I don't know.' Boyle climbed over the gate and he and Jack sat against the prickly hedge the cows coming towards them brave with curiosity. 'Your Mummy and Mark are going out to a place I really like. Ever since I was little like you, it's been my place and I only share it with very special people. That's all.'

'Mummy's special.'

'Yes of course she is.'

Jack leapt about, never sat still for long, and Boyle watched his straight brown legs in the pasture. He hadn't been to the island since Sean had gone and he didn't think he could bear to go again. His hopes and dreams, ideas, were there, his special place.

'And the lake can be dangerous Jack,' he warned.

'Will it be dangerous to Mummy?'

'No,' said Boyle thinking that perhaps it would.

'Why can't I go?'

'You're too little.'

'I'm big!'

'Not big enough.'

'When will I be?'

'Quite soon.'

'Dada said I was big enough.'

'What do you mean?'

'He's going to take me swimming. I have to get my face wet. I'm going to ride on his back.'

'When you're bigger.'

'Now!' insisted Jack, 'tomorrow!'

Boyle stretched his hand out for the boy and the child came into his arms, quite loving, natural. 'Would you do something for me,' he asked.

'Yes.'

'Don't go out with Dada, not just yet.'

'I want to.'

'Don't go. For me.'

Jack wriggled off his uncle's knee and 'shooed' at the cattle, 'I'll do something else for you,' he said.

Boyle smiled hopelessly.

'What else would you like?'

'It doesn't matter,' he said to Jack, 'never mind.'

They passed the remainder of the afternoon quietly, Boyle clinging onto it somehow, wanting to stretch it out, aware that every part of it was forming a memory that would later hurt, 'and then we, and then we, I had the feeling of . . .' At tea he made the little sandwiches with crusts off just as Aimee did, Marmite and peanut butter, poured the milk into the glass, put the biscuits on the plate. 'Children,' Aimee had told him, 'love routine, consistency, change upsets them.' If this was so then it was something that Boyle had not grown out of.

After this he gave the child a bath. His skin was soft, his stomach, still the baby protruding tummy denied by the schoolboy sturdy legs all bumps and scratches, and the hands so strong and wide, able to grasp and manipulate with ease. They had the fire engine in the bath and Jack ran it along the edge so that the sandy earth fell down into the water. Boyle washed him all over with lots of tickles and recited: 'Please remember, don't forget, never leave the bathroom wet. Don't do what you shouldn't oughter, little boys don't drink the water!' Nevertheless Jack sucked the flannel, splashed the bath mat and succeeded in getting his hair soaked. Boyle rubbed his hair with a towel, 'Mustn't go to bed with wet hair,' he remembered.

'I mustn't go to bed then!'

'Go on!'

'Shall I get Mummy's drier?'

'Do you know where it is?'

'You get it.'

'You come in.'

They sat on Aimee's bed, Boyle put his hand beneath her pillow. Her nightdress was creamy, slippery and soft. He blew the hair dry although Jack much preferred the hot air down the neck of his pyjamas. When Boyle kissed him goodnight he asked: 'Will Daddy come in?'

'Yes.'

'One more kiss then.'

Boyle gave several kisses.

'I won't go to sleep,' said Jack but he did, lying on his back with his hands palm up behind his head, flat out. Boyle went to his own room and looked through the window but there was no sign of the boat, without the diversion of the child's questions his heart felt sick.

Desmond saw it all: small fields and white blackthorn hedges, the town pubs and the new car showrooms, the hotel 'done up' since he left, the chalets by the lough shore, saw it all in a 'not stopping' tourist sort of way. All quite attractive but rather irrelevant to him. No tug at his heartstrings as he rounded the familiar bends, just a view out of a car window, a glance at his father, the same but older, driving in the middle of the road.

His father talked quite eagerly as they drove the distance from the hotel outside Enniskillen and out to the big house, talked and explained; the crater in the road that had been the culvert bomb, the library and the post office, 'gone', who had died and who had been killed, the family on a shopping trip to another part of the province, blown to smithereens, who had bought what and for how much, which parcels of land had 'gone the other way'. And Desmond noticed how the town now came out further than it had before, pretentious and ugly pebble-dashed bungalows dropped seemingly at random from the sky, the clean gravelled drives and serried gardens ending in the traditional stone gate posts. Philistines he thought and dismissed them as his father had done the death of Ferguson, the arrest of Maguire; a friend of Boyle's he had said with just a slight inflection in his voice.

Drawing closer to the border they passed an army observation post, a sandbagged mound covered with camouflage material where some joker had put out a sign, 'Waitress Wanted'. The grey of a police landrover, open at the back, swung past them and Dada mentioned Mark who he had so far apparently avoided meeting. 'A friend of yours at school I believe.'

Desmond remembered him.

'Coincidence,' he said.

'Don't tell me you disapprove,' said Desmond.

'Of the army? I do certainly!'

'But you'd be lost without them.'

'We're lost anyway.'

'You're not getting anti-British in your old age!'

'I'm not in my dotage yet,' replied his father surprising Desmond by the seriousness of his tone.

'You'd rather sort it out, fight it out yourself, is that it?'

'Not at all, not at all.'

'What then?'

'I never took a side,' said the old man.

'Sure, I know that!'

'I wouldn't like to be pushed.'

They drove for some moments in silence. 'They call it polarization,' said Desmond direct to camera in his special broguey voice. He turned the word over in his mind, examined it, exact but not emotive, failing somehow to bring to mind quite what his father hinted at. For Desmond had read about it of course, 'heard tell'. A different sort of troubles from the squeal of brakes and the ambulance sirens, the sensation of a large explosion or the hysteria of a running teenage riot. Softly, softly, polarization, it came about through organized intimidation, the hand on the shoulder, the kick aimed at the small of the back, the movement of the herd with all the blindness that implied, the erosion of individual, well-reasoned decision, free will and choice, a little insidious burrowing tic. Roddy would be interested in this, intimidation, terror, polarization, getting the bleeders by the balls.

'We should have gone into the Free State long ago,' Dada was saying. 'Long ago. Sure it's terrible altogether.

It's all changed, the town's changed. Nowhere to bury the hatchet but in some other fellow's back. A queer do altogether,' he said bitterly. 'Nowhere to bury the hatchet but in some other fellow's back!' he repeated as if he had thought the phrase often to himself. 'The army'll not stop it, not at all! No matter how many troops your government send over.'

'Not my government,' like Peter, Desmond on his own, not five minutes in the province, denied responsibility for the mother country.

'Is is not?'

'Of course not.'

'But you wouldn't come back now?'

'Well . . .' Desmond appeared to be considering the matter. He knew he would not come back, his father knew it too. If anyone had taken sides at all, Desmond had by leaving.

'Ah now,' said his father closing the subject, that neither would ever really open, 'Ah now.'

It all seemed so incongruous, almost melodramatic on such a lovely evening in such a lovely year. 'I expected you to tell me it was all a communist plot,' said Desmond on a lighter note.

'Tchh,' said Dada fondly.

They smiled. After four years apart they could still meet as father and son, mutual respect for two outsiders, no sides taken, and yet Desmond had the feeling that his father was reprimanding him just a little. Not really as impressed as he had appeared to be, playing up to the film crew in the bar of the hotel, standing a round of drinks to help them get 'acclimatized' he'd said. Although the eyes were now a weaker blue they were not unduly dazzled by the veneer of London glamour.

'And what's this film about then?' asked Dada mirroring his thoughts.

'It won't bother you.'

'I'll see that it doesn't.'

'They just want me,' Desmond ran his fingers through his

hair, 'to talk about the islands, the stones, that sort of thing.'

'Wouldn't Boyle be better doing that?'

'Well, he's bound to be in on it of course,' Desmond was aware of a little sweat of fear and guilt. 'How is he?'

'Ach!' his father threw his cigarette out of the window, his hand off the steering wheel and the car veering sharply to the right. 'He's himself,' he said 'one eye on the moon and the other at the bottom of the lake.'

'No girls?'

'Tchh,' was all his father said. Boyle was a throwback, or that is, he should have been thrown back years ago. Less than half a man.

'And the farm's okay?'

'What's left of it. A wee bit there and a wee bit here, not much doing, this EEC's a queer thing altogether.'

'You didn't lose any cattle in the fire?'

'Not at all. Old Shoey lost one when a helicopter thing landed in his field, buzzing around like big gnats!'

'And do you still swim out?'

'Certainly! I'm to take your wee lad out so he says. He's a grand wee cub Dessie, you should be proud.'

'I am. And Aimee?'

'Powerful looking.'

'She's settled in all right?'

'Sure she had the place cleaned up within a week. She's out on the lake with your man now.'

'Which man?'

'This soldier boyo.'

'Mark? Well it's nice for her to have some fun.'

'Aye.'

As they finally rounded the last bend and got their first glimpse of the lake, Desmond did remember the other times. Boyle used to close his eyes, lying out on the back seat on his way back from town, trying to work out where exactly they were, counting how many turns they had made from left to right. Desmond sitting on his father's knee doing the steering. Now he was too big, too heavy for his father and his father wouldn't want to take his weight, now it was his son he would take out on his back.

'Jesus they got a knock,' exclaimed Desmond indicating the gates and the gate posts now hanging hopelessly after the fire engine's rush.

'They did surely!' agreed his father getting back into the car. 'Well here we are then!'

Desmond looked up at the house, the house where he was born, the windows he'd looked through as the rain spilt, poured, sloshed, relentlessly down, season after season. The Wellingtonia he had climbed with his brother and the old fear, that irrational, unquantifiable, strange dread of Boyle came back to him as if the papers he had burnt in Bernie's grate would now rise dreadful from the ashes. He got out of the car and slammed the door with bravado that denied the sense of precariousness that filled him as he stood on home ground.

'A great mess the fire made of those!' said his father pointing at the sad line of burnt out shrubs.

'They'll grow up.'

'Not in my lifetime.'

'Come on,' he patted the old man on the shoulder, they were the same height now, 'a few more summers like this and they'll grow.'

'This is a freak.'

'They say the weather's changing,' said Desmond.

'They say a lot of things.'

Boyle wanted to say so much to his brother, he was nervous now and shy.

'He looks grand,' said Dada, 'look at him,' as if Desmond had just come home from school.

'I'm pretty wrecked actually,' said Desmond, the 'actually' coming across very English. 'Aimee's still out I suppose,' he turned to look out at the lake.

'Terrible isn't it,' said Boyle.

'Oh, I don't know, a bit of a mess I agree. Ah it's not so bad,' he gave his father a playful punch. 'A change is as good as a rest, you know. You've lost the trees but look at the view!'

'Come in, come in anyway. I'll make some tea.'

'Ach now, Boyle surely we can give the man a drink!'

Boyle on his way to the kitchen changed direction. They walked into the sitting room which was warm and stuffy, opened the windows.

'What'll you have?' asked Dada.

'A whisky.'

'That's the boy.'

'Boyle?'

'Please.'

They sat down in the unused room, Desmond slightly ill at ease and formal.

'Has it been very hot?' he asked.

'Fierce,' said Dada.

Desmond drank some of the whisky. 'I thought it might be cooler over here.'

'Not a bit of it!'

'The ground's very dry,' said Boyle remembering the abortive attempt at gardening, 'Oh, Jack's in bed by the way.'

'I must go and see him,' said Desmond but stayed where he was. 'He's okay is he?'

'He's fine.'

'I've got something for him, will I get him down?'

'Aimee said something about seeing him in bed, I suppose . . .'

'Ach get the cub down, Dessie,' said his father, 'get him down!'

Boyle poured himself another drink, shrieks of joy came from upstairs he and his father sat in silence until Jack came down in his present, a suit of plastic armour, a visor, a shield and a long bow, almost as tall as himself.

'You didn't give him a gun then,' said Dada laughing.

Jack, the bowsman, hovered at his father's side, dipped his fingers in and out of his father's drink.

Aimee and Mark touched as they pulled up the boat,

turned it upside down. Their hands and bodies touched as they walked up the steep garden, they bumped, touched, moving gently together. They could hardly have failed in such a romantic setting to confuse their emotions, pleasure and satisfied curiosity, the shock and delight of the new. For Aimee, the hand that reached out to hers was very welcome; a pleasantly experienced and gentle hand, a new hand, above all an English hand; for all she knew their mothers might well have played each other at tennis. All was right and, if not quite proper, quite properly done. But for Mark, almost unwittingly, it had been a transaction of a more serious nature. He buried his fear for that moment inside her. For a while he was free of it. The fear that kept him on his toes, turned the man into a soldier, for a moment he buried in her.

She embraced her husband smelling his usual evening state of semi-drunkenness, Mark beamed at Desmond too, what an absolutely tiny world, how very, very small!

'Look, I had no idea at all. Absolute surprise, complete coincidence!'

'How long are you going to be here for?' asked Desmond.

'Another month to put in.'

'You get plenty of time off then?'

'Well, it's slightly easier down here, this is my third trip actually.'

Dada was introduced. They shook hands, the old man got the soldier a drink.

So they sat in the last glow of the evening looking out through the sitting room windows, polished by the lady with the cloth, beyond the burnt out rhododendrons and out across the water.

Desmond patted the sofa and Aimee fell into it, leaning back laughing.

'A gorgeous day!' she said, she didn't care. She sat back and listened and looked. Watching her new lover and the older model come to grips, enjoying the enforced formality of their relationship inside the house away from the lake and the little island. He was relaxed, his shirt open, the strong brown arms, the shorts. Desmond by comparison resembled a snail recently released from its shell. He wore what looked like a new shirt, nastily too tight for him or perhaps still tucked together by the dozens of pins one finds in new shirts of that type. The collar and the cuffs were a different colour to the body, his hands were pale and freckly, his reddish hair dusty and thin. Really she felt a growing revulsion and a sense of surprise that she was actually his wife; that the family in whose beastly bosom she now sat was in effect, her own! She should of course have been Mark's wife. The attraction of opposites that had drawn her to Desmond in the first place had long been superseded by irritation. Mark she understood. The way he talked to Dada was smooth and easy, congratulating him on the prospect of the house, sympathising about the fire. He was confident and he gave her confidence, he knew how to behave.

'And you're going to deprive us of Aimee's delightful company?' he was saying to Desmond.

'Not immediately, no. We're shooting the film this week, everything has to be done at a sprint, you know what the BBC are like.'

'I can imagine,' said Mark laughing although really he did not possess a great deal of imagination.

'How is it going to be done?' asked Boyle.

'I've got a script here actually: move Jack,' he picked up his briefcase (another new object that went unpleasantly with the shirt). He handed it to Boyle, 'It's just a working script. They want to leave it a bit loose and see what happens. I rather hoped we might have a look at it together after supper.'

Boyle beamed.

'Look,' Mark stood up, 'I really must be off.'

'Well look,' Desmond got up and took him to the door, 'let's get together, go out for a pint.'

'Not on the cards I'm afraid.'

'Oh of course, how silly of me, got to get acclimatized, I

haven't been over here for years. How about dinner sometime?'

'That would be lovely,' the soft down of Aimee's thighs and stomach came to Mark and made him smile, he'd lost his fear.

'Goodbye Aimee,' he said, 'Thank you for a delightful afternoon.'

'Oh no, thank you,' she said.

'Look, just drop in. I'm not sure when this filming thing will be over (why was he diminishing it now, calling it a 'thing'?) I expect we'll stay on for a bit now I'm here.'

'I'll drop in during the week. I usually find a moment.'

'Right, well . . .'

'Best of luck with the film,' said Mark getting into the car, 'it sounds most exciting.'

'It'll be a laugh anyway,' said Desmond waving goodbye. 'Extraordinary people,' he added somehow wanting to disassociate himself from it in front of Mark, his hero at school, as if filming wasn't really cricket, 'Goodbye.'

'Bye.'

Desmond needed to get his bearings. He wandered down the drive, dragged the hapless gates together after the soldier's car. The smell of the lake in the evening worked like a powerful nostalgia for him and yet how strange it was, unexpected. Fermanagh for Desmond had always been a place apart, somewhere one came back to which had absolutely no connection with anything else. Yet this time Aimee was here and Jack, Mark, Ivan and Clover, Ireland and England, the past and the present all thrown in together. It could have been fun if it had been like this, not so cut off, remote. Now that it touched the other boundaries of his life, it was easier to take, to believe in. The red cat slithered past his legs and he bent to stroke it but it arched its back, neatly avoiding his touch, and he watched it disappear into the grasses of the lough shore field: he felt the softness of the air on his cheeks, listened to the sound of roosting birds, the cry of the cockerel, the engine noise of motor boats far out on the water; yes he needed to get his bearings.

The shortness of the flight from one world to another always brought confusion but this was exacerbated for him by a sense of a gathering of the clans as if characters from several different plays, which in a way they were, now jostled impatient in the wings waiting to come on. Heading back he rescued Jack's toy tractor from the flower bed blowing off the dust, noticed the unopened packet of seeds. The Big House in the last sunshine; all of it had a dreamlike quality in which disparate elements merged in an apparently quite natural and simple way.

If it was a play there was tension in the dressing room. Boyle and Aimee behaving rather as if one or other of them had hidden the spirit gum and was refusing to give it back. Boyle was reading a book, Aimee knitting with a vengeance, the faded carpet stretching just enough space between them.

'What's the form tomorrow?' asked Aimee looking up, half in a world of wool.

'The form? We're meeting at the hotel.'

'What exactly will you be doing?'

'Well, it's a tight schedule, race around and get the pictures I suppose.'

'It's a film then?' said Boyle.

'I told you it was a film.

'No. You said . . .'

There was a knock at the front door. Aimee twitched in her seat at the thought of some grubby little hand on her knocker and went to answer it coming back with a pale blue envelope.

'What's that? What is it now?' asked Dada, tetchy and cross.

'For Boyle,' said Aimee.

Boyle crossed the carpet for his letter.

'Bit late for the postman,' said Dada, 'Tchh!'

'What's this, what's this?' teased Desmond roaming round the room.

Boyle put the unopened letter between the pages of his

book.

'Aren't you going to read it?' asked Desmond.

'Who's it from,' said Aimee counting her stitches, 'Wasn't that the little Maguire boy?'

'It's nothing,' said Boyle but it was, a letter from Sean, 'A friend of mine, he was doing his exams, I was helping him.'

'Where is he now?' asked Desmond conversationally.

'Crumlin Road,' said Dada.

'Where?'

'In jail,' said Boyle.

'Oh dear!' said Aimee, 'What's he done?'

'Nothing.'

'He must have done something,' said Aimee.

'No, I don't know. They found something on his land . . .'

'What's he been charged with?' asked Desmond.

'I don't know, possession perhaps, something like that.' Boyle was nervy, his voice wavered, keeping it light. Christ! keeping it light.

'Sounds nasty,' said Desmond.

'No. I don't think he was involved, not really.'

'Catch yourself on!' said Dada, 'Tchh!'

'He was intimidated,' Boyle studied the carpet, his face red, embarrassed now.

In the silence Aimee counted her stitches in pairs, 48, 50, 52 . . .

'Forced, you know . . .' Boyle appealed to his brother.

'Poor guy,' said Desmond. 'I wouldn't let Mark find out about it, I shouldn't think he'd approve.'

'Approve of what?'

'You getting letters from him.'

'You can get letters.'

'I'd watch it if I were you.'

'It's nothing to do with him.'

'Have it your own way.'

'I think I'll get an early night,' said Aimee packing away her knitting, longing to be alone, away from them, to think.

83

'Oh don't go up!' Desmond stretched for her hand. She squeezed it quickly.

'I'm tired, darling.'

'But I've hardly seen you. Come on Aimee, I've only been back five minutes!'

'I'm whacked,' said Aimee firmly.

'It's only ten o'clock,' he said.

'No. I've got Jack to cope with tomorrow. You'll hardly be on hand to help.'

Boyle wandered outside with his book, keeping the letter like a maid, to read it later in his bedroom. Dada also took himself off, the toe of his boot just by chance meeting Aimee's ball of wool and sending it scattering beneath the sofa.

Desmond poured himself another drink. 'Honestly darling,' he said, 'I thought you'd be relaxed after all this, weeks in the sun?'

'It's not easy to relax when one's totally responsible for a small child!'

'Come on! You've had Dada to drive you round, Boyle to help you.'

'For your information your brother has done his utmost to hinder me in every way.

'Aimee!'

'I mean it. He's utterly spoilt. It's quite exhausting.'

'I'm sorry,' Desmond was puzzled and surprised. 'He helped you today, with Jack.'

'Today, yes.'

'And when Jack was ill.'

'You can't understand because you haven't been here,' she said blaming him. She hadn't meant to argue, hadn't meant it at all but now her mood of pleasure had been spoilt, she felt miserable, drowning in her marriage.

'Well, I'm here now,' Desmond put his arms round her but she stood holding herself fiercely, unbending in the embrace.

'You've no idea how difficult he is!'

'Jack or Boyle?'

'Both of them. Boyle's worse than a child, complete idiot.'

Desmond's earlier vision of amalgamated plays and players, of happy union between England and Ireland had already begun to disintegrate, prove itself to be meringue. 'Keep your voice down for God's sake.'

'I don't care if he hears me, he knows what I think.'

'Calm down!' said Desmond raising his voice.

'I'll tell you something,' she said coming towards him, whispering the old stage whisper, pointing with her pretty face, 'he burnt that boat, and the boathouse, he did it all deliberately, I saw him go to the shed!'

'Don't be ridiculous.'

'I don't care what you say, I know it.'

Desmond sank back into the sofa getting beyond her reach. 'Boyle would never do a thing like that. He loves this place, he'd never do anything to damage any part of it. It means everything to him.'

'That's what you think!'

'Oh go to bed!'

'I will. Just keep an eye tomorrow, you watch, you'll see.'

'You don't expect me to take this seriously?'

'I do actually.'

'Come on!'

She looked sullen.

'What's the matter with you, Aimee,' said Desmond trying again. 'I thought you'd be glad to see me . . .'

'I'm glad to see anyone in this dump.'

'What's up?'

'Nothing's up,' he irritated her beyond belief, 'I'm tired that's all,' she kissed him quickly on the cheek, 'night.'

'Goodnight.'

Aimee was asleep by the time Desmond eventually made it to bed. He lay beside her listening to the silence, as if the tape had stopped, all the noise of London wiped off; he lay beset by the sort of feeling of some unknown anxiety, when one has worried and checked that the plugs are out, the headlights off in the car, and yet . . . At one point he sat bolt upright in bed. I'm going to get killed here, he thought, something's going to happen. His mouth went absolutely dry. I might get killed, in a pub! Jesus! Or shot by mistake, shot because I look like someone else. He rubbed his hand over his face, I might get shot because I am myself! Of course there was no reason why he should be shot, of course there wasn't. His family had never, in their long history in the house, never had anything to do with politics. They were apolitical if anything. His father had acquaintances rather than friends but Desmond was sure he had no enemies. Perhaps Boyle, that letter, this involvement whatever it was with the suspected boy, it could be unhealthy in a multitude of ways. No. That was impossible, he wasn't that stupid!

Desmond lay wide awake. It was just the sort of thing that happened though, the niggling irony of life and all that. Blameless individuals, on holiday – his heart plunged – 'bumped-off!' Now he was being stupid! But there didn't need to be an enemy or even a motive come to that. Religion was enough, Jesus he didn't even practise a religion. He was really frightened and rather wished he did. What if he saw something, by accident, an accidental witness! He swallowed in horror.

Desmond and Boyle argued over the film script that lay closed between them on the breakfast table. Boyle's face, with a look of reproach like that of a beaten dog irritated Desmond, but determined to be jolly, to defend himself and his project, he lit a fag, feeling grim himself that morning, grim but pleasantly professional. It was all new to Boyle, not so much perhaps a reflection on the script but the idea behind it, the fact, previously glossed over, that Desmond's interest in the stones was purely professional, a commercial venture rather than a personal interest. Boyle could help him; if Boyle needed wooing, he would woo.

'You don't like it do you? I must say I didn't think you would. It's not completed of course,' he picked it up,

'there's room here for all sorts of other stuff . . .
'Sure it's crap altogether.'
'Hang on. Hang on. It's only a working script this. The idea was to leave the whole thing loose, Ivan's like that, improviser extraordinaire, it depends a lot on what they see. I think you could really help us, if you'd like to.'
'I don't want anything to do with it.'
'Why not? Honestly I didn't think you would object that violently. What's wrong with it.
'It's rubbish, fairies, banshees . . .'
'That's Clover's department, Ivan's wife, she is a bit, you know, into the old occult. But actually I think it's got a place, don't you? Pagan traditions, that sort of thing?'
'I do not.'
'Well, I assure you that's nothing to do with me, half of it won't go in anyway. I think the problem is, you've got to understand,' Boyle was sullen, Desmond kept trying, 'understand that it has to be popular.'
'It says documentary.'
'I know it says that but they, well, they'll have to dress it up a bit . . .'
'The Celtic twilight!'
'Don't be like that. Hang on! No need to be so bloody negative,' he lowered his voice again, 'please.'
'Yeats!'
'What's wrong with Yeats? I think Yeats fits rather well.'
Boyle looked positively furious as if he knew exactly what was wrong with Yeats in this context or in fact in any other, Desmond was annoyed, looked at the clock above the mantel, was anxious to be off.
'Look. I've got to go. Why don't we talk about it in the car, we haven't got time to get it sorted out this minute.'
'I'm not coming.'
'Don't be stupid. They're expecting you.'
'No.'
'Christ!' Desmond picked up the script and prepared to leave the house. 'Look,' he said, 'You're being a snob about it all, aren't you? Do you want to put Fermanagh on

the map, do you want everyone to know about these extraordinary stones or don't you? You did the articles in the first place . . .'

'Not in this way,' Boyle insisted.

'Are you coming?'

'I am not.'

Desmond hovered for a moment, he really had to go. Boyle was sulking. 'Fuck it then,' he said and walked out.

Driving down towards the town, the script bouncing on the back seat of the car, Desmond felt apprehensive, cross. It was a bit over the top in some ways, that was Clover's fault. Ivan's critical faculties bent double by his desperately fashionable, faddy wife, a skinny brown rice and sandals type who'd been a researcher on one of his early projects. The fairies, little people, were very much her department whereas Ivan was more interested in his first idea of counterpoint and also getting down to the basics of what these standing stones and figures were all about, the emotions, passions they inspired, represented, more on the lines of Boyle's article, probably the right lines he thought grimly. The stones had been, still were, powerful symbols, as strong as the Christian cross. Centuries on, here they stood, around and on these tiny islands, undisturbed, revered. Of equal interest and importance was the fact that they continued to be manufactured, so cleverly that many were extremely difficult to date. In Derrylin there was a male bust outside a pub, dated about 1850, by a stone mason called Maguire. Formerly it had stood on the other side of the road next to the masonic lodge and was known locally as 'King Billy'. Another, with a similar face and narrow curled moustache now stood in a rather undignified position on the septic tank beside the former RUC station in Mullyneeny townland, this could either have been folk art of 18th, 19th century or might even be pre-Christian. Undoubtedly there were secrets here; mysteries, a tradition that continued right into the twentieth century in this remote, poor, countryside must mean something. If it needed fairies, Yeats, to get the message across, and

Desmond, full of Boyle now, doubted that it did, so be it. Desmond had his own part to play, narrator, playwright, having got this far along the road he would not let Boyle's delicacy, Boyle's mutterings about the dignity of the stones diminished by the whisper of Yeats, and Lady Gregory, get in his way. So, the vision of Clover in dark glasses and drooping Indian skirt, Ivan, rather paunchy outside the office, without the benefit of his well-cut suit, did not deter him as he arrived, a little late, in the car park of their lakeside hotel.

Desmond had a chat with Ivan and half an hour or so later they turned up, Ivan, Clover, Desmond plus the film crew from Belfast in an attempt to get Boyle to join them at least for this first day. Ivan was greatly impressed by Ballyross finding the whole tumbling heap of it 'marvellous, evocative and atmospheric', Aimee providing cold drinks was pleasantly impressed by Ivan, Boyle, like a stone himself, stood very much to one side.

Losing the battle they set off with much shouting of instructions and revving of cars. Dada came out of the house.

At this point a young boy, twelve or thereabouts, appeared from the shore, up to the house in search of 'Mr Boyle'.

'They're off then,' said Dada to Boyle, 'Hardly an early start.'

'Yes,' said Boyle who was the cause of it.

'You could've gone with them?'

'I . . . This is Sean's brother, Dada, Aidan Maguire,' said Boyle instead, unable to hide the boy who now stood beside him.

'Pleased to meet you,' said the boy.

'Ah yes,' said Dada, 'Yes.'

'I'm up to help with the gates, sir.'

'Ah.'

'We'd better get to it then,' said Boyle in some embarrassment. 'We'll keep Jack with us. Go on into the back shed there, Aidan, and see what you can come up with.'

Boyle felt nervously for Jack's hand, Dada obviously did not approve.

'What are you up to now?' he asked disparagingly.

'I said, to mend the gates.'

'Tchh!'

'I'll help him find the tools,' said Boyle but his father held his arm.

'Jesus, Boyle, get a grip on yourself. You should have gone with them. Not mucking around here, a wet nurse to two children!'

'I told you. I want to mend the gates. I'd rather stay here.'

'But you'd enjoy it, you could tell them a thing or two.'

Boyle looked sulky, he might have been eight and his father just forty.

'Ah, just as you like!' said Dada, 'But you're a fool man, a great fool, an idiot,' there was no exclamation to what he said, he had said it all before.

As they were coming back with the tools, Dada reappeared carrying a bathing towel.

'Me, me!' yelled Jack.

Boyle held tightly onto his nephew's hand.

'Tomorrow boy,' said Dada.

'Promise! Promise tomorrow!'

'Tchh!'

They spent all morning at the gates. Boyle was happy because the boy was Sean's brother, contact at last. The boy had no idea that this man loved his brother, even Sean didn't know that. Boyle had only known it when it was too late. He would never take anything for granted again, ever. Like Jack's little parcel of love. He'd had a go at Desmond for picking Yeats because Yeats was a romantic yet now he whispered, 'I have spread my dreams under your feet; tread softly because you tread on my dreams.' 'Get a grip,' said Dada but of what, onto what? What could he hold onto that wouldn't slip away?

They worked all morning at the gates, Jack throwing stones at the Texaco cans, ping, ping; worked all morning but hardly made any impression at all. They re-hung the worst side but the buckle in it meant that, hung back properly, it no longer shut. Someone would have to come out, take the whole enormous thing off, get it hammered straight somehow. The job was far too big for them but doing it brought solace.

'What will Sean do?' asked Boyle as they carried their tools back to the house admitting defeat. 'What will Sean do?'

'Stay where he is sure,' replied his brother very matter of fact, 'What else can he do?'

'How are your parents taking it?'

'All right,' the boy looked into the distance and it was hard to tell whether he was really as unperturbed as he pretended.

'How are you getting on with the farm without him?'

'All right.'

Boyle didn't want Aidan to go now but saw no way to keep him there.

'And you. Do you get on well at school?'

'Wee buns!'

'You're very like your brother.'

'That's right.'

'I wondered, Aidan, shall I give you a letter for him, would that . . .'

'Okay.'

'Could you hang on? If I write a note?'

'Surely.'

Boyle hovered by the doorstep not so sure. 'Watch yourself with Jack now,' he said warningly. 'Be careful now if I go and write this won't you.'

'I will surely, Mr Hamilton.'

'I'm trusting you now.'

'There's wee ones at home.'

'Oh. Fine. Well just give a yell if you want me.'

'Okay.'

Boyle sat in the dining room. Aimee had asked him to clear it out, a shameful waste of a beautiful room she'd said.

He'd agreed of course but he hadn't started yet. He rolled some paper into his typewriter, just sat. He thought of Sean but the only word that came to him was 'help'.

'I haven't been well since you left,' he wrote.

My brother is over making a film. You might have enjoyed it; my brother Desmond, his wife, Jack their son. They have become friends with a British soldier. We had a fire down by the lake, I expect your mother told you. It's good to have Desmond home, we haven't talked yet, he thinks it's nothing to do with him. I'm not up to this, I feel if you came back – There hasn't been a drop of rain since you left nor a whisper at all of wind. The lake is very calm. Aimee and the soldier have borrowed your boat! They went out to the island. Every day is blue, very bright, very, very clear, no thunder or anything and then black at night with lots of stars. When I was at school I went to France and the stars remind me of that. You see them as if you've never set eyes on them before. It's almost a shock, high and bright in the sky, fabulously cold. I'm absolutely alone here since you left although Jack, my nephew, has given me a lot of pleasure. I feel alternately terrified and calm; the red cat disappeared after the fire but the bastard soon came back! Naturally I'm delighted to see Desmond, do you remember him? I doubt I shall see much of him. Please Sean, I long for your company, on my own like this there's nothing left, I feel so mad. I think it's getting through to me this 'throwback' thing. That I somehow lost touch with their reality is certainly true but Dear God, it wasn't deliberate. We used to talk, do you remember, and I said it was like being on a seesaw? With you at the other end it was all right. Now the place is full of people. If I seriously thought I was crazy, and that's a contradiction in itself, I'd do something about it. Just a little bit either way could tip the scales to some advantage. Dada recommends 'getting a grip' – but what on. Oh God! surely it's not very complicated. It's a simple little truth, Sean. I want to love but I can't go on much longer. There must be something mustn't there, this surely couldn't be it for me. I can't find anything soft. Only the stone, that's it. Not that I go there these days. That morning we were to meet I cycled out there feeling fine, thinking you would be there of course, expecting you, and then I blamed you dreadfully but I see now it wasn't your fault, not at all. I expect Desmond's there today.

Perhaps I should go away. I don't know. When you've no one to talk to it all gets bottled up. I told Desmond I didn't like his script, if he only knew how alike we are. I see it in those terms so vividly. As if this countryside, Fermanagh, should rise up and cry for what's happening here: all of it, the works! Tearing of hair, rending of clothes . . . some enormous demonstration, some frantic public display of grief and shame, anything rather than this quiet acceptance of terror and horror and blood. I hate it now, I hate the people. The red cat is first on my list. I watch him sleeping on the windowsill and I think, it would only take for me to get a stone, crush that proud head. Not that he ever really sleeps. Oh no. He would scratch and shriek and bolt and the stone fly out of my hand. That's it, isn't it. There it is.

Please, please write to me and do it soon. I'm giving this to your brother to pass on . . .

He slipped the paper from the machine and folded it in four without reading it through or adding a signature. Then he took an envelope and sealed it up. Beyond the window Jack rode past in his favourite position, on someone's shoulders, frightening Boyle for a moment as if the child had grown tall while he had been writing. He slid the envelope into his pocket and went out, blinking, out into the sunshine.

'I haven't kept you from your lunch I hope!' he said.

'Not at all.'

Boyle picked Jack up and kissed him, 'You love me, Jack, don't you, you love your Nunky Bee.' He held the child tight to him but Jack wriggled to get free. The boy looked at his feet in some embarrassment.

'I'd best be away now for my dinner,' he said.

'Of course,' Boyle had let the child down but still held tightly to his hand. There was a pause, a silence, a wait.

'Will I take the letter then?' said Aidan holding out his hand.

'No,' said Boyle patting his pocket. 'I didn't write. You wish him the best from me, will you.'

'It's our mother that writes.'

'Well, tell her then, to send Mr Boyle's regards,' he looked beyond the children. 'Not very pretty,' he said.

'What's that sir?'

'Nothing really. The army captain, a friend of my brother's. He says that. The Troubles you see, not very pretty.'

'If there's anything else you want doing, gardening, cleaning cars, going messages . . .'

'No, there won't be anything else.'

'You can ring us on the telephone, like Mrs Hamilton there.'

'Yes, of course, the telephone, I could use that, the 'phone.'

The boy stood and looked at the man. 'I'm away then,' he said uncertainly.

'Goodbye now Aidan.'

The boy turned and went down the garden and along the lough shore, back the way he had come.

The filming continued for several days, Boyle and Dada watching the circus from a safe distance. On impulse – and Ivan liked to work like this, it was dangerous like swimming but he did it – the boy's brother, Aidan Maguire was hauled in. Ivan claimed he looked positively Celtic, Clover that he was the spit of the young Jesus Christ; in any case he was used to row back and forward to the islands with Desmond in the stern, sulking a little because Aidan, the weather and Ivan in particular had denied him the anticipated pleasure of the Aran sweater. Knowing he was on camera he composed his face to portray what he hoped resembled the burden of wisdom and experience, the struggle of a creative man in his most productive years and above all, the thinker and the Irishman, the patriot.

Boyle did not take part, he watched from his position at the nursery window with Jack. Looking beyond Aimee and Mark in the garden and out to the lake, Boyle understood that even in perfect summer weather and without acts of a malicious god, filming was not straightforward but involved instead a repeated motion of backwards and forwards like darning, like a dance. They started early in the morning, stopped briefly for lunch and continued late into the afternoon in what appeared to be a race against time but was actually an attempt to get the pictures 'in the can' before Ivan, who had adopted a flamboyant straw hat, fainted or lost interest. Desmond's part in the film had dwindled until he had only one line to speak: 'Summer, the sail gathers, perfect peace!' and he even had to say this over and over again as the helicopters spinning overhead knocked out his now perfectly modulated Irish 'R'. He saw little of his wife or son. The former looked well and tanned but seemed strangely besotted with sport. They passed each other always on the way to somewhere else, she with a racket or shuttlecock, a brand new box of balls. As Desmond struggled to get out of bed early enough to greet Ivan at the door he remembered the advertisements for the modern British Army, all skiing and skindiving, and remarked to Boyle how magnificently Mark had risen to the challenge.

All too soon it was over, the crew returned to Belfast, Ivan and his wife to London, all traces of them gone and Desmond, miserable, like a child left behind. Although he knew that he might easily have manufactured an excuse, might even have returned with them if he wanted to, unfinished business kept him where he was; where he was at this moment was on the lawn, Jack in bed, watching Aimee and Mark spring and dart in pursuit of the shuttlecock.

Mark was generous to the point of irritation. He was fair and he was reasonable, an unimpeachable sport. They had tried to pull Desmond into the game for a doubles but it hadn't worked. Mark had played with Aimee who was the weakest whilst Desmond and Boyle staggered and sweated condemned to the 'hill end'; Boyle not even trying, Desmond infuriated when Mark hit him obviously 'easy' shots. So now they watched instead.

'Sorry,' said Mark when he hit a good shot she could not return.

'Sorry,' she replied missing it.

'Seven twelve,' he said breathlessly, 'you serve. Have that one again.'

'Sorry.'

The game wasn't interesting if you weren't playing it and hardly riveting when you were. The brothers watched in silence and Mark and Aimee played yet another point, yet another match. 'Rather well matched,' as Dada had said going down for his second swim.

'Will we have a drink?' asked Desmond unable to face watching any more.

'Okay.'

They went back up to the house, Desmond feeling heavy and flat, deflated. Without Ivan and Clover, that severed feeling he always associated with Ballyross returned. Ivan had said that they'd established a very good working relationship, and that he had enjoyed it all immensely. Whether they had enough there for forty minutes was another question . . . working relationship . . . Desmond poured the drinks, Aimee was using the sitting room floor for sewing so they drank in the dining room. Boyle occupied himself with what she had asked him to do, collect up and shift all his 'stuff'.

'You beast!' Desmond heard Aimee squeal through the open window.

'You utter beast!'

'Come on, Aimee, get to it.'

'Oh, I've had it,' she said sighing, flopping on the grass.

'Come on,' encouraged Mark.

'All right. But you start.'

Desmond watched as if mesmerized. 'Whoops. Sorry!' the shuttlecock stuck in the net.

'Jesus!' he closed the window, 'I can't stomach it!'

Boyle continued to shuffle about among his papers, his files, his paints and pictures. It didn't seem to worry him. Desmond sat on the arm of the old chaise longue looking disconsolately at the already familiar view. He felt wrecked although he'd done nothing for hours but sit, nothing since they left. Perhaps it was a reaction to all the hard grind that had filled the last few days, but he felt sapped, the heat perhaps.

'Doesn't the heat annoy you?' he asked Boyle.

'What?'

'The heat. Doesn't it get you down?'

'A bit.'

Boyle seemed impervious to everything. He had picked up some papers now, writing and sorting them out, absorbed. Ivan had liked him but he'd never found out about the articles, that at least was a relief. In any case they hadn't made much use of them in the event, they had just been a starting point, Boyle's work, an inspiration. He felt a bit cross with them all; with Ivan when he thought of this, his ideas had hardly got a look in and using the Maguire boy in his place for the 'voice over' still rankled. Recording him just because he, Desmond, had according to Ivan, lost his accent. He knew one shouldn't get upset about that sort of thing but it did hurt. He felt, well, he felt exploited. They'd exploited him rather, they really had. He rose and got another drink. Beyond the window Aimee and Mark were now both on the same side of the net sitting in the last of the sunshine.

Boyle waved his hand dismissively and Desmond wondered how he could read, write with someone else in the room, how he could concentrate.

'Do you think I've lost my accent?' he asked.

Boyle did not reply.

Desmond went up to him; he would be answered, it mattered to him. 'Do you think I've lost my accent?' he repeated.

'A bit.'

Desmond yawned, longed for movement; Dada to come back, Aimee and Mark to come in, he was bored, bored, bored. Beyond the window Aimee and Mark were still chatting, Boyle wrote. He could go out and join them but why should he, he wouldn't. Stuff them.

'Well?' he asked Boyle. 'Do you think we've been exploited?'

Boyle put down his pen. He hadn't heard the question and looked up blankly.

'The film,' said Desmond doing the charade mime for it.

'I don't know what you're on about. I'm trying to write.'

'What are you doing anyway?' asked Desmond looking over his brother's shoulder and balancing his glass on a pile of uneven papers.

'Careful!'

Desmond put out his hand to steady the glass at the same time as Boyle, between them they spilt it.

'Now look what you've done.'

'Sorry! Only taking an interest.'

'Well I'd rather you didn't.'

'I'll mop it up.'

'No. Leave it,' Desmond leant over and started rearranging the sodden papers. 'Get off!' said Boyle standing up. 'I'll do it, please. Leave it.'

'You're touchy all of a sudden?' said Desmond, like Dada now, refusing to leave the papers alone.

Boyle snatched them from him and held them close to his chest. Desmond laughed. 'Come on! Let's have a look,' he took a bunch, smoothing out the folds.

'Leave it. It's nothing!'

'Letters?'

'Leave me alone,' Boyle's tone had changed, 'For God's sake!' he said, his voice full of panic, 'Leave me be!'

Desmond withdrew. 'All right, all right!' he said trying to make light of it. 'Honestly!' He went back to his chair with what was left of his drink, eventually Boyle sat down again though he looked pale, shaken. 'Really!' said Desmond like a terrier now. 'What a fuss! What have you got there that's so precious?'

'I told you it's nothing.'

'You're like a bloody baby,' said Desmond, 'Honestly!' But Desmond had achieved his point, got things moving, Boyle gathered the papers in his hand, a huge bunch.

'Why do you get so wired up?' asked Desmond.

'You wire me up.'

'I do not!'

'You do, you always do, always did.'

'I hardly ever see you. I just wanted to talk that's all.'

'You wanted to talk.'

'Yes?'

'I was working.'

'I just wanted to see what it was that's so bloody precious.'

'Yes, it is precious,' said Boyle standing still the papers in his arms. 'You don't know,' he stammered his face quite pink, 'You don't know what precious is, you never did. You don't understand the meaning of the word!'

'What do you mean?'

'You haven't got a clue have you?'

'What?'

'I'm going, I'm away.' Boyle gathered up what was remaining and left the room.

'Oh, do what you like!' said Desmond. 'Jesus God Almighty,' he put his head in his hands feeling exhausted, 'What a bloody fuss!'

'Am I disturbing you?' Mark, his head round the door, obsequious as a chicken.

'No. Come on in.'

'What's the matter with Boyle?'

'No idea!'

'Something's put the wind up him.'

'Everything puts the wind up him.'

Mark smiled needlessly. 'Mind if I have a drink.'

'Please. Help yourself.' Desmond watched as the soldier

poured himself an unnecessarily large whisky. There was a limit he thought, even to Irish hospitality.

'And where's my pretty little wife?' he asked.

'Changing.'

'Oh,' Desmond yanked his feet from the arm of the chaise and turned to face Mark who now sat relaxed in an armchair his long legs, brown, slim, crossed at the ankles in a pair of perfectly white Dunlop sports shoes. 'Changing for dinner I suppose?'

'Sorry?'

'Nothing, nothing.'

'They've all gone back to London I see, the BBC chappies.'

'Yes.'

'Went pretty well, I gather.'

'Gathered from whom?'

'Oh you know, I just thought . . .' he paused to drink his whisky, 'When are you off then?'

'I've hardly been here five minutes.'

'Oh. I rather thought you were going back with them?'

'No.'

Mark blushed. He actually blushed; Desmond smiled, 'What are your plans?' he asked.

'More of the same I'm afraid. Work as usual.'

They drank for a moment in silence, Desmond was beginning to get drunk.

'Odd,' he said, 'Odd though isn't it. Odd,' setting his pale eyes on his new victim, 'You know what I mean, "work as usual/business as usual", a bit of a euphemism don't you think?'

'Not really.'

'Come on!'

'No, I don't think so. After seven years "as usual" is what it is.'

'Grim though, don't you think?' Desmond went on, 'if this is usual? You will admit that surely?'

'Certainly it's grim,' said Mark serious in his white sports shoes.

'And yet you don't seem to mind,' persisted Desmond. 'It doesn't bother you, you don't mind.'

Mark had had this conversation, or versions of it, before and found it tedious. 'I simply do a job.'

'That's all.'

'That's all.'

'Opinions,' insisted Desmond, 'I can't believe that people in the army don't have opinions, views. Or perhaps you all have the same opinions. Surely you must be frightened?' tried Desmond remembering his own fears.

'Of course.'

'And – frustrated, all this "as usual" bit. I mean you're not getting anywhere are you?'

'I wouldn't say that.'

'What would you say?'

'Softly, softly catchee monkey . . .'

'The bloody jungle. Ah,' Desmond leant forward on the chair.

'Just a phrase,' said Mark moving uneasily in his. The Irish were bores when they drank, he wished Aimee would come in.

'A rather significant phrase I would have thought?'

'It's just a phrase . . .'

'Ah but phrases are important aren't they. If you're in the jungle that makes us the natives,' Desmond pounded the arm of the chaise with the flat of his hand as if it were a drum, 'oompa, oompa.'

'Come off it, Dessie,' said Mark embarrassed but Desmond was clearly not in the mood to 'come off it'. Mark looked at his watch and finished his drink, 'Phrases are your business,' he said.

'And what's yours?'

'Sorry?'

'What's your business? Over here. What business is it of yours?'

Mark got up. 'I think you understand that as well as I do.'

Mark towered above Desmond in his white feet and Desmond withdrew for the second time that evening,

'Okay, okay. Have another drink. We natives weren't made for this heat, it makes us argumentative.'

'I ought to be going.'

'Have a drink,' the drink was making Desmond sweat, 'This damned heat!' he said.

'Made our job a little difficult, your film,' confided Mark, 'going all over the place and that boy. You know his brother's in jail, I suppose?'

'So?'

'I just thought I'd warn you.'

'Thanks.'

Aimee appeared looking lovely.

'Going out?' asked Desmond.

'No.'

'Why all this fuss then,' he caught her skirt between his fingers, the waist was on elastic, he gave it a tug.

'Stop it Dessie!' but she laughed so that Mark could see her white and even little teeth. 'Why are you all in here anyway?' she asked, 'Look at all this stuff, and Boyle's got his papers all over the kitchen table. What's going on in this house?' she laughed again.

'You tell me,' said Desmond.

'Look, I'd better be going,' said Mark.

'Oh don't go,' pleaded Aimee who had made all that effort, the bath oil, the perfume, the mascara, just for him.

'No. I must.' He stood up and put his glass down on the dining room table. Desmond did not get up although Mark almost waited for him to do so, awkwardly he moved towards the door.

'Aren't you going to see him out?' asked Aimee.

'I think he knows the way,' Desmond was on the Cresta Run, sliding down towards depression. 'Perhaps not enough for forty minutes,' he thought, hell! hell!

Mark was still in the doorway. 'What has got into everybody?' trilled Aimee lightly.

'Long hot summer,' he said, smiling, and when they smiled at each other the join between them pulled taut.

'Perhaps we should all pray for rain,' said Aimee. They

walked to the front door through the chilly hall. Yes I feel it, she wanted to say, this thing between us pulled tight.

They kissed at the door, 'I could see you to the gate,' she whispered. 'I'll walk down.'

'All right.'

He left and Aimee returned briefly to Desmond. 'You're drunk. Honestly how could you be so rude?'

'It's my house.'

'It was awful, I was really embarrassed.'

'Good.'

'I'm going for a walk,' she said.

'Good,' he replied as she walked out and closed the door, 'Good.'

Supper was grim. Hardly a word except 'salt' and 'pepper' was spoken in the now perfect, bright kitchen. The air was leaden with unspoken reproach. Neither Boyle nor Aimee was speaking to Desmond, neight Aimee or Desmond was speaking to Boyle; Dada, whom they might all have spoken to in turn, did not show up.

It was a rule with Aimee never to lower herself and she stuck to it that night. She would not argue with her husband in front of Boyle, would not let the side down, in any way. The closing of the bedroom door however was the signal to begin.

'I was really shocked,' she said.

'Oh don't be so wet! I didn't do anything.'

'You did.'

'I refused to show him to his car, to see him off the premises.'

'You were extremely rude,' she was taking her clothes off, shaking them, folding them across the chair, neat, efficient, angry. He noticed that her breasts were almost as brown as the rest of her body, but the line where her pants crossed her hips was enticingly white, a Plimsoll line of desire. And he decided he wanted her, watched her from the bed as she brushed her hair furiously away from her forehead, 'I knew the minute you came in,' she was saying,

'That you'd be arguing.'

'We weren't arguing! He wasn't.'

'Why were you arguing that's what I want to know? Why can't you be civil. A lovely day,' she brushed. 'A beautiful summer,' brushing again, 'and all you can do is argue.'

She got in beside him and he leant across to her, 'Not all I can do,' he said.

'Oh leave me alone! Honestly Desmond, you can't behave really badly one minute then expect me to make love to you the next.'

'Why not?'

She deflected this. People who behaved badly deserved to be punished and she would certainly punish him. 'I just have no idea what got into you,' she said leaning on her elbow.

'Nothing got into me.'

'That's just it,' she said grimly, 'exactly.'

It wasn't the devil that entered Desmond, it was Desmond himself. 'Even if you don't like him you can at least be civil,' she said, and when he didn't reply, she went on: 'Anyway, I know why you're sulking, because they made a fool of you!'

'Who?'

'Ivan and that Clover woman, death on a mopstick.'

'They did not!'

'It was perfectly plain to me.'

'Look, I don't want to discuss the film.'

'No, I shouldn't think you do!' she exclaimed knowing that she was getting to him now. 'You made an absolute ass of yourself, slavering around Ivan like a dog!'

He might be tired but he couldn't sleep. If he was a dog, then Aimee was a bitch. Hell! Hell!

He'd promised her a holiday but that was a bit doubtful now. Really he hadn't made as much money as he'd expected, well, one spent so much in London, it was impossible not to, even a cup of coffee cost . . .

He nudged her, 'Aimee?'

'What?'

'Shall we go away on holiday?'

'What?'

'You know, on holiday. We could go off together, leave Jack here if you like.'

'I'm not leaving Jack here,' she said into the pillow.

'I don't see why not.'

'Anyway I'm having a holiday.'

'But a proper holiday Aimee.'

'Can I sleep now, please?'

He lay on his back trying to forget the white of her bottom. Everything seemed such a bloody mess. Perhaps he ought to get back to work, get down to his Irish play, get away from idiots like Mark and Boyle. There was something that had struck him a few days ago, one night? Something about Boyle but he couldn't remember now, can't have been important. He racked his brains, but he couldn't think of it. Something he'd said or implied. The old horrors of the night, the black of the August sky, the black dog on his back. Oh sleep! Whatever it was about Boyle he had forgotten it, oh sleep!

Betty Ferguson had spend the night with her sister in Enniskillen. The doctor had given her a massive dose to knock her out so that, although she was awake by six she still lay in the strange bed past eight am, flat out. In her mind, which felt like sodden cardboard, now she too struggled both not to remember and to forget. One could argue that these strong sleeping draughts really weren't fair. Under their influence the truth, that first her husband and now her son, the wee lad, her boy, the pet, were dead, was wiped out; this was fine because it let her sleep and sleep, well sleep heals, like sea water, it has a power. But the doctor couldn't be there when she emerged, woke up. He had done his best but she would eventually have to go through the shock of it all again, the shock of remembering what one has been dosed up to forget.

Everyone at Ballyross was horrified, shrank from it, listened to it several times on the news, felt the need to have it repeated. Betty had been on tranquillizers, valium, although they didn't say that on the news. Well a lot of them took it, to get them through, tide them over a shock, a bereavement. Her youngest boy, Kevin, had got hold of them somehow, killed himself on the yellow pills, an accidental overdose.

'In black and white on the radio,' said Mrs Devlin. 'What a to do' and 'How frightful!' A new wave of repulsion and unhappiness surged through the county, the province as a whole now used to destruction, havoc and death, mourned on. Some said the child hadn't much to look forward to anyway, just Jack's age but what would life have held for him? His father murdered and his mother wrecked and bitter. He wouldn't have inherited the farm with all those elder brothers, joined the security forces perhaps, kill or get killed himself, gone on just, they said, when he got older, gone on just to fight another day. And yet nature was untouched! That August morning was as beautiful, as perfect as the morning before. Some said that Betty would be off now, move away, get right out, but Dada didn't think so, knew better. These people, he might have said, stick to their ground or more precisely, to their guns. Come hell or high water they went on, dogged and divided hanging onto their land rather than let it, 'go the wrong way', no she would continue and in a way, survive. An ordinary woman with an old-fashioned and rather harsh hairstyle, the shoes and matching handbag that she'd seen, then wanted, had 'put by' that she'd worn to one funeral already. A dab hand at baking, clever with flowers and a member of the embroidery guild, she stood in the front line now flanked by politicians, policemen, publicans, and priests; all one in death and the distraction and negativity of mourning. She would of course carry on. Squeeze the liquid foundation carefully from the bottom of the tube and colour her pasty face, dust lightly with the powder puff, kiss automatically at the piece of tissue to 'set' her lipstick, brush the collar of her suit and look at herself in the overmantel mirror, 'A present from Portrush'. Her brother-in-law, her older boys, would bear the coffin. She had a daughter at the grammar school who would soon be 'going for' a teacher. Some said she'd never take another pill, that she'd been thinking of stopping, had cut right down, but that she'd needed them, 'sort of leant on her pills' they said. One suggested that she might go back on the cigarettes if she hadn't done as much already, but then they didn't know her well. She slept sadly now alone in the bungalow a gun beneath her single pillow.

Boyle said nothing when he heard the news that Dada had discovered the night before. Then they all heard it on the wireless, a fact among a list of facts. Other people who had died as a result of an explosion some weeks ago, the possibility of political settlement fading as the summer should be dying into autumn. The horror of such an incident, a near neighbour, allowed Desmond and Aimee to talk again, to pick Jack up, cuddle and kiss him, try, try, to keep him safe. Dada didn't touch his breakfast but it could have been a hangover, but they were all shocked and showed it, left the dishes in the sink.

'God, let's get out of here!' Desmond said to Aimee when Dada had left, Boyle gone out.

'It's terrible isn't it,' she said, 'Awful, really ghastly!'

Desmond sat where he was, shocked. 'It isn't really even the Troubles is it?' he said, Aimee making more coffee and sitting down beside him. 'Stay in here Jack, there's a good boy,' she sat him on her knee and fiddled absent-mindedly with the magazine that she had been going to read.

'I mean it's not just the Troubles,' said Desmond again.

'Indirectly it is.'

'An indirect hit.'

'That poor woman. God! Do you think I ought to go and see her, rally round a bit?'

'I don't think so.'

'I will if you like, if you think I ought to. I'd be glad to,' she said stroking Jack's hair. 'I'd like to do something.'

But Desmond shook his head. 'No,' he said, 'she's got plenty of relations, they'll look after her, she'll be all right.'

'You don't think we ought to show the flag a bit? She is a neighbour?'

Desmond drank his coffee. They had never had anything to do with neighbours, with anyone. 'No,' he said, 'leave it. Better in the long run.' Aimee looked down at the cover of her magazine, Jack's warm body on her knee. Desmond looked at both of them. 'What do you think of this holiday idea?' he asked.

'Oh Desmond, I can't think about holidays now, not at a time like this!'

'Okay. Not now. But would you like to, we can take Jack if you like?'

She looked doubtful, squeezed the child on her knee, the last thing she wanted was to spend any time alone with Desmond.

'But haven't you got to get back to work? I mean can you take a holiday now?'

'I don't see why not.'

'Well don't you think you ought to consolidate your success. I mean get in there with something else, you know, not let the eggs go cold?'

'Do you think so?' the idea sounded most appealing, she could be right.

'Can I get down now mummy?' asked Jack.

'Hang on,' she said.

'I suppose you could be right,' said Desmond thinking about it.

'I am right.'

'Will you – would you come back with me then?' he asked not knowing whether he wanted her to or not.

'I think I'd like to stay here till the end of the summer.'

'If that's what you want,' he said, perhaps he was relieved.

'Well, it would be lovely for Jack.'

'Please can I go now?' asked Jack again, 'Please!'

'Okay off you go but be careful.'

'And don't go on the drive,' warned Desmond feeling guilty now, protective, 'Grampa's moving cattle.'

'I'll only watch.'

'Okay go on then.'

Jack walked confidently in the now familiar house, calling for his uncle Boyle, along the corridor and peeping into the dining room now empty of his uncle's things, calling up the stairs. Getting no reply he went to go outside but his ears were caught by a strange, unplaceable and yet oddly familiar sound coming from the sitting room. He stood on tiptoe to open the door, turned the handle but it wouldn't budge. He put his ear to the key hole and heard the sound again. 'Uncle,' he called through the gap, 'Uncle Boyle! Can I come in?' he couldn't see him but he was sure he was in there. 'Uncle,' he called, 'Unnncle!' He set off once more down the corridor to the kitchen and back to his parents. Aimee was doing the dishes in a pair of yellow plastic gloves, Daddy was reading the paper.

'I can't get in,' said Jack.

Desmond held his finger on the column he was reading, looked up.

'I can't get in, Mummy.'

'But I thought you wanted to go out darling,' he was precious, she kissed the top of his blonde head.

'No,' he said insisting, 'in!'

'In where, sweetie?'

'In the sitting room!'

'Go outside then,' she said putting her gloves back into the suddy water and when he still stood there added, 'I expect Uncle's in there working.' She turned back to the sink, washed a cup and a saucer.

'He's crying,' said Jack.

'Don't be silly.'

'Mummy, mummy! Go and see,' he tugged at her skirt. 'Come and listen!'

'Desmond.'

'What?'

'Can't you do something?'

'What?'

'Jack says the sitting room door's stuck.'

'So?'

'Boyle's inside or something.'

'Boyle's inside crying,' said Jack.

'Uncle Boyle darling.'

'He's crying, Daddy.'

'Don't be silly.'

'You'd better go and see darling,' said Aimee.

'All right, all right,' reluctantly Desmond put the paper down, he was reading about the drought, 'No peace for the wicked!'

Desmond walked along the corridor with his son. 'I can't hear a thing,' he said, 'you monkey! Come on!' He tried the door in question, turned the handle several times unsuccessfully. 'Boyle?' 'Probably stuck' he said to Jack and ran his hand down the side of the door and stooped to see if a toy or some other small thing had become wedged, stuck beneath it. He tried the handle again, it was locked. 'Are you in there, Boyle?' he paused, 'Boyle? Come on don't muck about, I'm trying to have my breakfast.'

A meek choking sound came from within, Jack smiled triumphant. 'Boyle, open the door for God's sake! What are you playing at now?'

'Go away.'

'Oh don't be silly. You can't go round locking doors!'

'Leave me alone,' came the voice, the tight, hard voice that went with the closed face – panic – the voice he had used when Desmond had spilt whisky on his papers.

Jack kicked at the bottom of the door.

'Open the door, Boyle,' said Desmond, 'Oh hell! Don't!' he said to Jack who was kicking at the door again. 'Stop it!' he said sharply.

Boyle did not open the door, Desmond returned to the kitchen.

'Guess what!' he said to Aimee who was still at the sink.

'What?'

'He's locked himself in! Brother Boyle has locked himself in the sitting room and is sobbing his heart out.'

'Don't be daft.'

'He is, I tell you, come and see for yourself.'

Aimee peeled off her plastic gloves, wiped her hands on her apron, hung the gloves over the gleaming arch of the tap.

'What shall I do?' asked Desmond.

Now Aimee began to pick the few dead heads from a vase of flowers, she shrugged, she sighed, 'Leave him to it if that's what he wants.'

'But he's crying!'

She flicked the pedal bin with her toes and emptied the dead heads out of her apron on top of the tea leaves and bacon rind, 'Really!' she said exasperated.

'Won't you come and say something to him darling, please?'

'I'm not going to spend my morning talking through a locked door.'

'Please Aimee. For me. He might listen to you!'

'Oh really! honestly Desmond you're such a child!'

'It's not me who is crying.'

'You're both children.' That's what was wrong with the Irish she thought, not mad, just plain childish, always squabbling, spoilt brats! 'Boyle. This is Aimee,' she said rather stupidly as it could hardly have been anyone else. She too had a voice for the occasion, a voice like a newly-clipped hedge, the voice she used when she was trying to get Jack to let her clean his ears with the corner of the flannel. 'Open the door please,' she said, quiet, firm, matter-of-fact.

'Go away.'

She rattled the handle of the door round and round. 'Open this door.'

'What are we going to do?' said Desmond, worried. Boyle had been worrying him, that's what it was.

'Go and look through the window, twit!' said Aimee suddenly thinking of it herself, 'I've had enough of it!'

'Oh right, how silly,' said Desmond, 'Come on Jack.' They went outside into the sunshine and looked through the sitting room window. Boyle was on his knees on the carpet, he had something in his hands. 'What's he got in his hands?' he said to Aimee. Boyle did not look up, perhaps he didn't hear them, his shoulders were shaking up and down with sobs. 'Oh, I see,' said Desmond. 'Looks like a bird.'

'Oh, really,' said Aimee and walked back indoors, 'How silly!'

Desmond tapped rather foolishly at the window, 'Are you all right?' he asked. 'Look, do let me in.' He tried one of the windows and found it open. Really it was very embarrassing, that's what he felt, embarrassed.

'Are you going to climb in Daddy?' asked Jack who hadn't found anything so exciting since the fire.

'Yes, I am.'

'Can I?'

'No.'

Jack began to whine.

Desmond climbed rather gingerly through the window. Jack cried outside tramping the dug flower bed.

Boyle's face was streaked with tears, his shoulders heaved, he sniffed. 'Are you all right?' said Desmond again. Outside the window Jack had lost interest but found the packet of 'Covent Garden White' which he now sprinkled on the dry, tramped earth.

Desmond tried to see what Boyle was holding. It was a bird, looked like a blue tit, there were a few feathers on the carpet but otherwise it looked unharmed. 'What's the matter with it?' he asked, 'Is it dead?'

'Yes.'

'Come on, Boyle don't be silly. It's only a bird.'

'That bastard brought it in,' he said viciously, 'That fucking cat!'

'Boyle,' Desmond passed him and unlocked the door, 'It probably died of shock. Where's the cat now?'

'It went out. I tried to get it with that,' Boyle pointed at a paper weight that he had thrown and which had landed near the window, 'Oh God!' he said, 'Oh God' and rocked to and fro on his heels.

'It's just a bird Boyle, relax.'

But Boyle still cried, it was shocking. Tears welled from his eyes and spattered down his adult face.

'Let me have it,' said Desmond gently.

'No!' Boyle held the bird protectively cupped in his hands.

'Let me take it. I'll get rid of it for you,' but this was greeted by a fresh burst of awful crying. 'It's a bird, Boyle, a bird. Cats get birds, it's nature. That's what happens. Come on, give it here.'

Boyle handed it to his brother, they both shuddered as the warm feathers passed from hand to hand.

Desmond took some time to put the bird in an ashtray and cover it with his hanky. He was very embarrassed, really a bit shaken. Jack came through the door but he took him firmly by the arm, 'Run along Jack.'

'I want . . .'

'Run along!' he said firmly pushing him back in the direction of the door, 'Mummy wants you. Now, go on!' He re-locked the door and poured them both a drink. 'Look,' he said to his brother, 'have this. You mustn't get so worked up, it's absurd.'

Boyle drank and shuddered again. In the order of things he was absurd, tears just poured down his cheeks. Desmond was unsure what to do. He supposed he should put his arm around his brother, tap him gently on the shoulder; some sort of physical contact was called for, but he couldn't do it, shrank from it. Instead he said, 'Better now?'

'A bit.'

They both drank the whisky. Desmond looked at his watch. It wasn't even ten o'clock. 'What a morning!' he said in what he hoped was his normal voice, trying to get things back to normal as quickly as possible.

Boyle got up slowly from the carpet and slumped into an armchair, there were feathers on his pullover and he had removed his glasses making his face look oddly exposed, naked. He held his empty glass tightly in both hands. 'I've had it,' he said feebly, 'I'm cracking up.'

'Come on. Pull yourself together. You're fine.'

'I'm not, Desmond,' he looked straight at his brother but his brother looked away.

'You are,' he said. 'You're just upset that's all. It's all a bit upsetting. Nothing to worry about.'

'You don't know how worried I am,' said Boyle beseeching Desmond with his wet, undressed eyes, 'Oh God!' he said, 'I'm in a mess!'

'What sort of mess?' Desmond tried not to sound too sharp. Jesus, he was thinking, what now? Families! That boy Maguire or something, 'What sort of mess?'

'You wouldn't understand.'

'Try me.' Aimee appeared at the window with a jug of coffee but Desmond gestured for her to go away. Boyle had bent his head again and the crying had recommenced. 'I would Boyle, honestly,' said Desmond. 'Try me, come on. You can tell me.'

'I can't.'

'Is it something . . .' Desmond was not quite sure how to tackle this one, 'Is it something about the fire?' he asked feeling his ground, 'the boat?'

'Not that.'

'What then?'

Boyle shook his head hopelessly. 'It's all right,' he said, 'It's all right,' but he was crying, crying.

'I can't really help unless you tell me what it is,' said Desmond pouring himself another whisky.

'I can't pull through it any more, he muttered, 'everything's all over the place, I can't place anything, work it out, it's all up and down . . .'

Desmond was confused.

'There's no soft in my life, d'you see? No soft.'

Desmond did not see, did not really want to. 'Calm down,' he urged, 'take it easy. You're probably under too much strain. It happens to all of us,' he said, 'We all go through it now and then and you know what you're like,' he added thinking of school.

'You mean school don't you?' said Boyle.

'No. I didn't think of school. What I mean is, well, you must relax, you've got to. It's strain Boyle, overwork, the Troubles, anything and everything. Things mount up. Little things on top of bigger things. The fire, the Fergusons' child, the bird. It's the straw that breaks the camel's back.'

'Or bends it.'

'What do you mean?'

Boyle fiddled with his glasses, put them on, his face changed dramatically as he did so, he looked better. He said, 'Sorry, sorry. Let's stop this, I'm all right.'

'Whatever you want. I'm here if you want to talk. I'd like to help you Boyle, you know that,' now was the time to pat his shoulder but again he froze from the act. 'I'm sure it's nothing,' he said, 'You need a good rest. The heat's getting to all of us . . .'

'It's bound to break soon,' said Boyle thoughtfully looking forward, ahead, at nothing.

'Of course it will, bound to. It's the hottest summer for twenty years.'

'The back I mean,' continued Boyle, still looking out at nothing.

'I don't quite . . .?'

'What you said, the camel's back.'

'Did I? Oh I see, yes, absolutely. What you need is a good long rest.'

Boyle looked down at his hands. 'I don't sleep,' he muttered.

'That's because you're overtired,' tried Desmond desperately. It struck him that this conversation was like talking to his son, to Jack, except that he touched Jack, quite naturally, held him.

'And there's no one to talk to.'

Desmond sighed, a sigh worthy of his wife. He could hardly ask Boyle to sleep with them as he might have asked Jack. It was all very difficult, very tricky. 'You ought to get out a bit more,' he suggested, 'Go into the town more, the bookshop, the museum. Out on your bike, cycle round to the island like you used to, go and see your precious stone.'

'It's precious to me.'

'I know. I know. I'm sorry.'

This 'sorry' wasn't big enough, the 'sorry' for the film, the gap between them, age, experience of life, prospects, yawned wide open.

Boyle studied the carpet now, his eyes flicked from the window, the view, to his hands on his lap, to the carpet where the old red loop merged with the crimson, appearing to study each place on which his wet eyes fell, looking for something to hold on to. 'What will happen when you go?' he asked his brother, 'What will happen when Dada goes?'

'Goes where?'

'Dies.'

'Nothing, nothing'll happen. I mean you'll go on here, if you want to that is,' he looked at his brother, he could hardly offer to have him in London, he hadn't the room for one thing. 'I don't see why anything should change,' he said as gently as possible.

'Will you be here?' Boyle was beseeching, begging, Desmond was considerably embarrassed, his armpits actually prickled with nervous sweat.

'On and off,' he said.

'You couldn't stay?'

'You know I couldn't stay,' the word, 'couldn't', seemed to stretch out into the room, to run from window to window, wall to wall.

'I'd be on my own then,' said Boyle refusing to adjust his gaze although new tears were starting to run now beneath the rim of his spectacles.

'You've got friends.'

'I haven't.'

'I'm sure you have, Boyle.'

'Don't start again,' said Boyle. 'Let's leave it, please.'

Couldn't was only applicable to that room wasn't it? Couldn't and nothing, nothing, nothing.

'You wouldn't like to leave here would you?' said

Desmond. Boyle shook his head. 'Anyway this is silly. There's no point worrying about something that hasn't even happened.'

'That's what I do worry about, all the time.'

'About Dada?'

'About things that haven't happened. I'm sort of waiting for them. Sort of paralysed waiting, can't move, do anything, else.'

'Dada's good for a few years yet!' said Desmond in the tone of the scout master to the tearful cub, 'He's as fit as a fiddle, fitter than both of us put together!'

'Not Mark though,' said Boyle moving his head to look straight at his brother.

'Mark? What's Mark got to do with it?'

'I don't know.'

Desmond pursed his mouth, now he waited.

'He's fit, that's all,' said Boyle.

'Is he?'

'Yes, he's fit.'

'Well what's it all about, don't you like him or something?'

'Do you?'

'I don't like or dislike him.'

'You were friends,' said Boyle with a definite note of accusation in his voice.

'Years ago, yes.'

Desmond would talk about Mark if that was what Boyle wanted, firmer ground this, he thought, and was much relieved. 'I think we've both changed,' he said quite happily now, 'gone our separate ways.'

'And yet come together again.'

'That's just a coincidence.'

'Yes, I suppose so.'

For some time Desmond had wanted to pull Boyle out of the chair so that he was mightily relieved when Boyle stood up of his own accord.

'Feeling better?'

'A bit.'

'Good,' another chance to touch him came and went. 'I'll bury this for you,' he said in mitigation, assuaging his guilt.

'Will you put it in the flower bed?'

'In the flower bed? Here?'

'Please.'

'Out here?' Desmond looked beneath the window.

'If you would.'

'Okay, anything you say.' Desmond tried a laugh, 'Right,' he unlocked the door with a flourish.

'Thank you,' said Boyle, 'for the chat.'

'Any time!'

'I am glad you're here.'

'Yes,' said Desmond standing away from him to let him pass, jollying him through the door, 'It's nice for all of us. I'd better get back to my breakfast, I feel quite tipsy after that drink! What are you going to do?'

'You don't have to watch me like a child.'

'Okay, calm down, I just . . .'

'I'm going to lie down.'

'Good man. That's it, take things easy. And don't take it out on the cat!' he joked as Boyle walked slowly up the stairs; he may not have heard, in any case he did not reply.

Aimee was doing her hands. They'd really got quite rough since she'd been in Ireland and she'd been meaning to do them for some time. She rubbed gently at them with cuticle cream on the cleared kitchen table, massaging with the cream, smoothing it around her fingers.

'Breakfast over?' asked Desmond coming back into the kitchen, putting his arm round her neck.

Aimee sniffed, she had a good nose for smells, she didn't smoke. 'You've been drinking Desmond, ugh!'

'Medicinal drinks and brotherly love,' said Desmond.

Aimee had finished the creaming, screwed the top back on the bottle and begun now to file her nails, carefully, skilfully, up, across, down, up, across, down. 'All I can say is thank God Mrs Devlin wasn't around!'

'Why's that?' asked Desmond watching the practised action of the emery board, 'What's it got to do with her?'

'Nothing. That's just it, so embarrassing. He's a complete baby,' she said looking at him firmly.

'Ach now, don't be too hard on him Aimee. He's really in quite a state.'

'About the bird I suppose.'

'Yes, about the bird, about everything.'

Aimee continued to file, nail after nail, looking at each one, comparing one hand with the other. 'Quite frankly I can't see what he has to worry about?' she said, 'He has absolutely nothing to do all day.'

'He thinks a lot,' said Desmond defensively.

But thinking was contemptuously spat out. 'Thinks!' She put the file down on the table and shook the bottle of nail varnish up and down. 'Thinks!' Perhaps if he had something to do, a decent job . . .' the ball bearing in the bottle went up and down, 'he wouldn't have so much time to sit around and get all moody.'

'Aimee!'

'No, I mean it,' she said starting on her thumb nail with three deft red strokes, 'I mean it darling. It's pure self-indulgence. That's all it is. He's got absolutely nothing to occupy his mind.'

'What would you suggest?'

Aimee shrugged, 'Well . . .'

Desmond lit a cigarette, he felt sorry for Boyle now, he poured two cups of coffee from the percolator.

'Where is he now?' asked Aimee.

'Up in his room.'

'Oh.'

Desmond pulled on his cigarette, a bit of toast would have been more sensible. 'I suppose you have got a point,' he said reluctantly, 'about the job I mean. I did say to him he ought to get out more, into the town, get about a bit.'

'Mmm,' Aimee had lost interest rather. She waved the polished hand in the warm air.

'He says he hasn't got any friends,' said Desmond.

'He must have friends,' scoffed Aimee starting on the other hand. 'Surely?'

'I don't know. I suppose I'm rather out of touch.'

'Well, it's not your fault, darling,' she said looking at him, smiling.

'No, you're right. But he is my brother.'

'Your elder brother. For God's sake Desmond he's not a baby, you can't run after him all the time!'

'But I do feel a bit, you know, responsible really.'

'Oh don't go on about it.'

'But I'm worried Aimee, honestly. You don't know what it was like in there,' he insisted like a man just returned from the front line, 'I think you're being just a bit hard.'

'No, Desmond,' Aimee shook her pretty head, 'I'm not being hard, I'm being realistic. There's no point mollycoddling him now, when in a few weeks, days maybe, you'll be back in London. It just doesn't work.'

'I suppose you're right,' said Desmond with the thought that he had said this just before. He stared into his coffee feeling unhappy and uneasy. It had been, whatever she might say, an upsetting morning. 'I keep thinking about that poor woman,' he said.

'I know,' she answered, 'Ghastly!'

'Why do these things happen?'

'Who knows?' Aimee looked hard at her nails in the silence. 'I think these need a second coat,' she said. 'What do you think?'

'Very nice,' he said absently, 'very pretty. Have you noticed, Aimee, how awful things always seem to happen in beautiful weather?'

'No, I haven't actually.'

'They do,' he said, 'honestly. It was a day like this when mother died.'

'I'm sorry.'

Desmond felt surprisingly near to tears, he was shaken, shocked.

'You're getting maudlin,' she said, 'You shouldn't drink on an empty stomach.'

'Why are you – why do you have to be so tough all the time?'

'I'm not tough at all. I'm being sensible. You know what you're like when you drink. I certainly do! What's the point in getting yourself all upset. There's nothing anybody can do.'

'You're sure of that?'

'Of course I am.'

'But you don't think I should do anything?'

She sighed. 'About what? Mrs Ferguson, Boyle?'

'About everything. Come back over here for good. Play my part.'

Aimee was at the finger tip waving stage again, it helped to dry them quickly, 'Playing a part is just about it,' she said astutely, she knew Desmond, 'It wouldn't work. There's nothing for you here.'

'I don't know. I keep feeling, I should do something. Not just for Boyle, for the country.'

'Come on!' but Desmond looked stubborn.' Okay, tell me. What would you do if you came back here?'

'Nothing I suppose.'

'Exactly!'

She got up and put her things away in a smart beaded bag, a special bag for nail things, the conversation was over. She kissed him lightly on the temple, 'Could you do those spuds darling?' she said, 'I've done my hands.'

'Yes. Fine. Where are you off to?' He didn't want her to leave him now, he wanted comfort, something.

'I've got to see if Dada's going into town. I've got a mound of stuff to get.'

'What for?'

'Tomorrow night.'

'What's happening tomorrow night?'

Aimee was taking her shopping bag from the peg on the door, she checked her handbag for her wallet and cheque book, desperately casual. 'I told you darling,' she said apparently preoccupied, 'Mark is coming.'

'What for?' asked Desmond making a face.

'Supper!' She kissed him again as she would Jack, a glancing uncommitted kiss. 'I'm sure I mentioned it.'

'I don't remember. Can't we put him off?'
'Why?'
'Well . . .' Desmond tried to think of a reason.
'You haven't arranged anything else, have you?' she said, cross now, a definite change of tone, a cold wind blowing through the heat, 'Honestly you are exasperating, I told you yesterday!'

'No, I haven't,' said Desmond sulkily. 'Couldn't he come some other time sweetheart? I don't think Boyle's really up to it,' he tried.

'Boyle needn't come.'
'Well, does Dada know?'
'Yes.'
'He doesn't mind?'

Aimee had the door handle in her little red and white hand. 'Don't let's make an issue out of this, Desmond. Why should he mind? Please don't make something complicated out of something very simple. Mark is coming to supper tomorrow night,' she continued spacing out the words so there could be no misunderstanding. 'It's all arranged and I can't put it off. Now I'm going to find your father.'

'Tchh!'

'Bugger Mark!' said Desmond as he did the spuds. The thought of sitting round the dinner table entertaining Mark was the last thing he wanted. He was quite sure she hadn't mentioned it, he wouldn't have forgotten something like that. Perhaps Boyle was better off without women, he thought, without friends. Turning disgusted from the sink he noticed the dead bird in his handkerchief still on the dresser. Oh Lord, he thought, suppose I'd better get rid of it!

'What is it?' asked Jack, coming in on mummy's express orders to 'go' to daddy. He lifted the hanky, 'It's dead,' he said.

'Yes,' said Desmond distractedly. 'Poor old bird. I'm going to bury it, do you want to help?'

'Yes please!' They went out into the sunshine. 'Whereabouts, Daddy!'

'Boyle says he wants it in the little flower bed beneath the window, here.'

'Will it grow?'

'Of course not, silly!'

'Why plant it then?'

'Bury, not plant. It's what you do with dead things. Bury them.'

'Why?'

'Oh I don't know. Because it's healthier. You have to bury dead things.'

'Who says?'

'I don't know Jack,' it had been a long morning, 'just let me get on with it.'

Jack was delighted. 'How deep is it going to be?' he asked, watching his father with the trowel, stabbing ineffectually at the hard earth.

'Too deep for you to dig it up again, monkey!'

'Do you bury monkeys?'

'You could.'

'And gorillas?'

'I suppose so.'

'Elephants?'

'Jack, haven't you got something to do?'

'But do you, daddy, bury elephants?'

'I don't think so.'

'What happens to them then?'

'Please Jack, honestly I don't know.' By now he had made a small hole. He popped the bird in. He felt silly doing it, stupid.

'Are you in a hurry?' asked his son.

'No.'

'Why are you rushing then?'

'It's not a very pleasant business, that's all.'

'Mark says that.'

Desmond finished with the bird and sat back on his haunches.

'Does he?' he asked.

'Not a pleasant business,' said Jack, standing very

straight and mimicking the accent rather well. 'He said it to Uncle Boyle when they were looking at the boat. Boats aren't a business are they, Daddy?'

'I expect he was talking about something else.'

'Aren't you going to put a cross up?'

Desmond left the graveside and picked up his son, 'Birds don't have crosses and don't ask me why not!'

'Why?'

He put the boy up on his shoulders as Boyle had done once, 'Why are you always asking why?' he said.

Jack giggled, 'Put me down! Put me down! Why why, why why, why, why,' he chanted.

'You are a wild, bad wee boy,' teased his father, putting him down on the gravel, 'Now what shall we do?'

'Where's mummy?'

'Gone shopping.'

'Why can't I go shopping in Ireland?'

'You just can't.'

'But why?'

Desmond held up his hand, 'Don't start again, please! Now what are we going to do?'

'Swim?'

'Not just now, darling.'

'Please!'

'Not today.'

'Where's uncle?'

'Up in his room.'

'Is he ill?'

'No.'

'He is ill sometimes. Mummy says he's sick.'

'Little boys shouldn't listen to grown-up conversations.'

'I'm not little!' protested Jack, 'I'm bored!'

'Do you want a walk?' said his father.

'If uncle comes.'

'Okay, I'll give him a shout!'

They stood back on the lawn and called up through the open nursery window, 'Jack and I are going for a walk, do you want to come?'

'Okay.'
'Great!' said Jack.

The days of August, the third month of drought, followed a recognisable pattern, dawning high and blue, clear cut with almost a seaside freshness and then changed, by ten or eleven in the morning, into a different heat, a heat that pulsed beneath a lower, deeper sky: a wet and humid heat that lay along banks and hedges and hovered low above the fields where cows flicked their tails to move the flies about; for the flies, so close to the lake, only moved and settled, moved and settled again. It was clammy sticky weather, typical of late August except that it was, or seemed to be, unbreakable. The freshness had long departed, the leaves, so various in spring, were now simply green, worn and dusty. A break from this humidity would have been natural but it didn't come. Farmers sniffed for a breeze bringing rain but there was no breeze; in and around Ballyross it was weather as usual.

Boyle and Desmond wandered down the drive beneath the heat, down to the gates so buckled by the engines, the petrol cans and weeds unscythed, now higher than ever. Only Jack had energy, did 'Nangaroo jumps' way ahead of them.

'Did you sleep?' asked Desmond, solicitous.
'Not really.'
'I think a walk will do you good.'
'I'm all right!'
'A pity about the gates,' said Desmond, snubbed.
'Oh yes. I tried to have a go at them.'
'You should really get someone out, a professional.'
'I will.'

Desmond looked hard at his brother not sure whether he was sulking or perhaps still 'not himself', it was difficult to tell. In any case after their intimacy that morning, the confessional, he felt rather awkward, ill at ease knowing really that he'd failed him in the sitting room in a situation where perhaps it would have been difficult to win. In desperation they both turned to Mark. 'Aimee has invited Mark to supper.'

'Oh yes?'

'Apparently.'

'Oh.'

'Aimee arranged it all, told me, just there now in the kitchen.'

Boyle blushed and Desmond noticed, 'What's the matter?' he asked.

'Nothing. Nothing at all, sorry.'

'Do you want to sit down?'

'I'm not ill! I'm hot!' Boyle rattled out the words in quick succession. 'I will sit down if you like. We usually stop here.' Jack, on cue, jumped onto the five-barred gate.

'It's very close isn't it? Perhaps we'll have a storm,' Boyle looked up at the sky, quickly, up and down again. 'No. Maybe not. I don't think so.'

Desmond rubbed his eyes. Things were not going frightfully well. Like a bad rehearsal the dialogue was forced. Perhaps it was unnatural anyway the two of them on a walk like this. Even as children they hadn't done much together, Desmond swam, Boyle cycled. And those links with childhood, how tenuous they seemed on this hot morning with Jack, a new child, playing and poking the verges with a stick, chatting away, quite happy.

They sat down in the field which smelt of wild honeysuckle and Meadow Sweet. Jack called from the gate; 'Look Daddy! Look!'

'Very good darling.'

'Look!'

'They seem to like ritual, to do things in the same order over and over again,' commented Boyle remembering how he had taken Jack down to this place over the past few weeks.

'Yes, he's loved being here,' replied Desmond giving thank-yous to a stranger. 'It's been good for him. He's adored it. It seems a shame to take him away.'

Boyle kept blushing. He felt the colour come and go in

his cheeks as if something was happening in his body that he was unable to control and that this was the outward sign of it, the warm flushes, the sweat. 'Oh,' he said, 'Oh well. You've decided when to go then?'

'Not really.'

The conversation fell again like a stone in a pond, drop.

Desmond wiped his brow, 'Shall we go on a bit? It's even worse sitting down. Go back by the lake?'

'Fine,' Boyle got up.

'Come on Jack.'

'No!'

'Come on!' Desmond was sharp with him and hoped Boyle didn't notice, it was too hot for children, too hot. Jack still played on the gate, Boyle chewed on a piece of grass, Desmond stared out across the open field, no inspiration came from the flat green, the huge blue.

'Come on Jack! We'll go round by the lake and then we'll be back in time for lunch. We might see Dada!'

At the suggestion of Grampa the child jumped down quite happily and ran ahead of them again.

'How are you getting on with Dada?' asked Desmond for something to say, 'All right?'

'Yes.'

'He's not hard on you?'

'No more than usual.'

'That's good.'

Each conversation seemed doomed to failure, like spinning a hula hoop starting round the waist, round, round, and then hopelessly down the legs.

They were walking now along the pebbles at the lough shore, 'Oh look!' exclaimed Desmond, 'There's a dragonfly. Look Jack, there!'

'Where?'

'There!'

'Yipee!'

A dragonfly. The graceful creature dipped just above the water. 'I can't remember the last time I saw one of those!' said Desmond nostalgically.

Boyle picked up a pebble and threw it into the lake; the fly shifted and departed as quickly as it had come.

'What the hell did you do that for?' Desmond cleared his throat much as his father might have done. They walked on. 'Mark mentioned going out to the island, to look at the stone.'

'Really?'

'Perhaps we could all go out there tomorrow night, you know, under the harvest moon. Might soften the blow a bit.'

'Okay.'

'I mean I don't relish the prospect of sitting down and talking all evening.'

'No,' agreed Boyle. His eyes searched the lake for the dragonfly; he saw it, it had come back. He remembered a line about it in an old 'I Spy' book: 'the most predacious of insects'.

'Do you remember Mark at school?' asked Desmond breaking into his observations.

'I do.'

'What sort of things?'

'He was popular, always with a crowd, a small crowd, select. A member of the sporting élite. Practical jokes.'

'Pranks,' said Desmond finding the right word.

'Pranks' that was it, the brothers smiled together, the word shifting their difficulties momentarily to one side. They reached the path that led back up to the garden; there was no sign of Dada.

'Sorry darling,' said Desmond remembering, 'he took Mummy shopping.'

'We saw the dragonfly!'

'Yes. That's the boy.'

They walked up through the garden. Dada was back, Aimee getting out of the Vauxhall, carrier bags of groceries.

'Perhaps we ought to play a prank on him, you know, on Mark,' suggested Desmond as Jack went running off to join his mother. 'Wave the clappers out at the stone, remember?'

It was a game they had played as children. Desmond's game. He would go out to the island with a girl or some friends from the town and Boyle, hiding among the trees, would wave the old football clappers, shout and groan and shriek, make what they called 'ghost music'. The boys would run off, the point of the game being that there was just a possibility that the girls would swoon into Desmond's eager, adolescent, freckly arms.

'I remember,' said Boyle who had sometimes been beaten up by the boys.

'Just a thought, that's all,' said Desmond, 'a bit of a gag.'

Aimee had abandoned a cardboard box of goodies on the gravel. Desmond picked it up and Boyle held the door open for him. 'Are you on for it then?' he asked, shouldering the box.

'Seriously?'

'Yes. Come on! He's such a wanker!'

'Okay, all right,' but Desmond had the impression that he wasn't really listening, hadn't really heard at all.

Boyle felt extraordinary during lunch, coming and going, switching on and off like a radio, swooping up and down like a bird. Although he felt he had been eating his plate of salad for some time, it did not seem to get any smaller. One minute he would chew and the next look down at his plate in mild astonishment, had to force himself to distinguish what was on it: mauvy-pink and thin, was ham. Curly green leaves, were lettuce. Round, hard, misshaped balls with peeling skin; potatoes. His knife and fork felt heavy and long, unwieldy and he had to concentrate hard to work with them at all.

The conversation swirled about him and he picked up bits here and there none of which made sense.

'Closed up, what a waste!'

'Sure we couldn't heat the half of them!'

'Mrs Devlin had quite a go in there, a lovely room, nice aspect.'

'Fruit salad? Boyle shall I take your plate?'

'No, darling. I'm just saying I don't want to see him climbing gates, those gates or any other gates.'

'Sure they have to cut their teeth.'

'Boys will be boys you know.'

'I'd rather he didn't learn through accidents.'

'Look at that poor Ferguson child.'

'Poor wee Betty.'

'The mother has herself to blame.'

'Oh, won't you have coffee? Cheese?'

'And there's a fierce gap in the hedge at the well field. A whole crew of them got up last night and marched off up the road to Maguire's.'

'Come on, I'll take the wee cub.'

'Get some decent trousers on you.'

'He'll be scratched to pieces.'

'Mrs Devlin's coming in of course.'

'I know it's not her day.'

'I've changed the day.'

The dragonfly, remembered Boyle, passes the early part of its life at the bottom of the pond. It walks and climbs but cannot swim, it drives itself through the water, jerking, forcing water out violently through an opening at the tail end of its body. After some time it will leave the water and climb onto any suitable object. Its skin splits down the back and the adult dragonfly crawls out. At first its wings and body are small but they soon expand although often many hours or even days must pass before the colours acquire their true brightness.

'Are you going to eat that? I must get organised. I'm sorry, I need this table.'

'Everything's already upstairs,' said Boyle defending himself. He'd cleared the dining room table, cleared it! 'All my stuff's upstairs,' he replied.

'Boyle, you're miles away,' she said.

'I could wash up?'

'Thank you but I get on quicker on my own.'

Boyle went upstairs to the nursery, he'd stopped that old automatic turning to his own room; things had changed and he'd got used to them; it was Aimee's voice at each mealtime not the wireless, Desmond and Jack were helping Dada, the cows were in a different field. He lay face down on the bed, pressed his face against the pillow. He had always cleared the table, now Aimee stood at the sink, the yellow plastic gloves hung on the arch of the tap. 'Very much taking up the reins,' Desmond had said as if the house were a horse and carriage, something that moved. I taught Jack to climb the gate, he thought. 'Cross your hands when you get to the top, like this. No. Like this.' Mrs Devlin came on Wednesday, now she comes on Thursday. 'I changed the day.'

Boyle turned over on the narrow bed, opened his eyes. The nursery and Desmond's bed empty. The curtains depicting Noddy, Mr Plod, Big Ears and The Skittles hanging quite still in the warm, slow afternoon. Not moving. And here is my work, he thought, here in the nursery. He undid his shirt, the heat was stifling, the 'phone rang and he listened to Aimee's quick, light steps, the quiet closing of the door. He rolled in anguish on the bed. 'Shelanagig' he whispered. The word was out, 'She, She, Shelanagig!' He saw it scrawled large and hot in dark wax crayon, he bit into his pillow. Words came to him then up and up. 'Wantonly,' she behaved wantonly. He thought of her neck and shoulders and remembered an afternoon with her almost as if it were a picture in a scrapbook; 'Boyle and Aimee in the kitchen before the fire'. Ah, before the fire, before the fire. Take me back to before the fire . . . 'Have you finished with your bowl? Pass your bowl please. Thank you, I can manage quicker on my own.'

'Help me,' said Boyle to the pillow, 'help me.' He rocked himself on the bed, but Desmond will pay you back he thought. 'Desmond will pay you back,' he said out aloud in the language of the playground, the long and alien dorm, the shame of the wet bed, the fear when he'd blocked the basin. His housemaster had given him a rubber plunger. It made a sucking noise like the lake, that's what it reminded him of so far away from home; kissing the mud, sliding up the mud, kissing the mud, kiss, suck, suck.

'Suck,' came the voice then.

'Suck, suck,' said Boyle.

'What are you after exactly?'

'Love.'

'And you didn't get it?'

'No.'

'They're frightened of you, aren't they?'

'Yes, I believe they are.'

'But you've got it sorted out now?'

'I think so.'

'It must be a relief to know now.'

'A relief to know' repeated Boyle:

> 'A relief to know nothing's going to work
> Nothing is going to work.'

Boyle surveyed his belongings, his papers brought up from the dining room. Bundles of papers, some paper clipped, some stapled, some bound, some held in folders, some in files. It should go in sequence, on Desmond's bed, he thought, but it didn't work out like that at all.

Going to the first pile he wrenched it free of its bindings and threw it in the air. It was a big gesture, it made a mess. He pulled at the other papers, tore at the books, tossed them in the air. The papers fell and he walked over them with his bare feet, he scrumpled them beneath his toes. What he really wanted was to do something to them, not rip them exactly, spoil them, spoil it all.

Opening the nursery door he tiptoed onto the landing, down to his old room. That's what he wanted, the drawers from his chest. He took out the largest drawer and stretching his arms across it, began to carry it back to the nursery. He staggered across the landing. Aimee was briefing Mrs Devlin. 'If you could give this a good polish.'

'Powerful shame, them wee marks,' that was Mrs Devlin.

'Mmm. We could cover them up, strategically placed table mats.'

'Mmm,' echoed Mrs Devlin doubtfully.

'There are some table mats, aren't there?' asked Aimee as if questioning whether Mrs Devlin used a toothbrush. 'Oh dear me. They are in a ghastly state! Just pop them into the kitchen and I'll have a go at them myself.'

Boyle stood still and listened to this conversation uncomprehendingly, unable for the life of him to remember the place, the people or the context. Who was it talking about table mats and why?

He got all the drawers into the nursery. That was much nicer, much better for everybody, everything together. He found what he wanted without any bother, hair stuff and shaving cream, talc, presents from Christmases long ago. He opened one bottle and took a sniff and tipped it all over the floor. Then another. Despite the open windows, the room began to smell very strong. Now he squeezed a tube of Palmolive onto the floor, across his papers in a white sausage streak, he punctured the tube with his nails and the white stuff smeared his fingers, he wiped his hands on the paper, arms full of them covered in the sticky stuff. 'Bitch!' he said as he vandalised hours of close set work, the dotted 'i's and the crossed 't's, 'Life's a bitch, bitch, bitch!' When he had exhausted all the bottles and powders and tubes he looked in the other drawers; rugby shorts and shirts, shoe laces, vests and here, ah, the two huge wooden football clappers they had been sent from America. He wiped his hands on the curtains and then sat at the foot of his bed amongst the remains of all his work, cradled the clappers carefully in his arms in case they might go off spontaneously like a gun. 'I hid in the bushes by the stone. No, of course I didn't want to! It was his idea. I sang ghost music when the girls came, they clung to Desmond! He paid me for it. One and six, blood money. I can't remember if I saved it up or perhaps I threw it away or lost it. Desmond was frequently out of funds, perhaps he stole it back?'

Boyle tried hard to think of Sean but could only think of Desmond stealing money. Children were allowed to apologise, say 'sorry' and 'I didn't mean to', and 'I promise I

133

won't do it again'. Adults had less leeway, Sean could make little headway being 'sorry' for the gun, Desmond didn't apologise for anything. Boyle looked at the mess he had made of his bedroom and thought, 'You'll be sorry for this young man!' An orgasm of destruction he thought, and giggled helplessly, lay wide-eyed, sated, 'Mummy look, no hands!'

Lying on the bed, eyes closed, things went small, went big. Desmond was a baby and Boyle was six years old, his mother cross with him for singing in the bath. Mind out, be careful, don't wake Desmond, shhh!

'Och isn't he the real wee dote, Mrs Hamilton.'

'Would you look at those wee fingers, gorgeous so he is.'

'And how's wee Boyle then?'

'Boyle adores him.'

'Is that so, do'you love your baby brother?'

'I do.'

He didn't go down for tea or supper. He didn't mind if he never ate again, he wasn't hungry, not hungry at all. He peeped from the low-barred windows at Aimee wheeling the trolley gingerly across the lawn for tea beneath the Wellingtonia. Later Desmond shouted up to him, 'Tea?' and it was easy to shout back, 'Not for me.'

'Do you want a cup brought up?'

'No thanks. I'll be down later.'

Deception needn't be dramatic. Boyle lay back in the horror of torn up, fouled-up papers, broken picture glass, books with their backs bent right off, broken backed books. Quite simple really if one puts one's mind to it. Later on he left the nursery and locked the door behind him. With the clappers wrapped carefully in his shirt he went quietly, and quickly from the house in his bare feet, got out his bike as if he'd cycled it just the day before and set off down the drive and through the gates. 'I never got the child's seat,' he remembered, 'it doesn't matter now.' In the hurry to leave, on the impulse, he had forgotten his shoes, the pedals reminded him, hard and strange to the soft soles of his feet as he set off down the road.

'How did you get on in the dining room?' asked Desmond as they brought the tea trolley in again.

'Oh very well. She's quite a good worker if you approach her in the right way.'

'From behind,' he said and put his hand underneath her arm, round feeling for her breasts.

'Not now, Desmond.'

'When?'

'Jack'll see us.'

'Bugger Jack!'

'Oh, there's the 'phone.'

'I'll get it.'

'No. You push this down to the kitchen. I'll get it.'

Desmond unloaded the trolley and ran some water into the sink. She wouldn't sleep with him, the bitch!

She was on the 'phone for some time, he heard her laughing.

'Who was that?' he asked.

'Mark,' she answered shortly, 'Do you smell something funny?'

'No.'

Aimee sniffed, 'What on earth is it?'

'I can't smell anything.'

'That's because you smoke too much.'

'I can smell you,' he said, coming towards her again.

'Every cigarette takes five minutes off your life,' she said, squirting the Fairy Liquid nastily into the sink. 'There you are,' she pushed away from him. 'Please, Desmond, give it a rest, I've got to put Jack to bed.'

'Mmm, bed,' he said, his wet hands slipping down the shoulder straps of her sundress.

'Stop it!' she said, pushing him away again.

He stood back flushed and annoyed, 'You wouldn't mind if Mark did it I suppose?'

'Don't be so stupid.'

135

'He doesn't, does he?'

'Of course not!' She came towards him then, a bit frightened, and put her hand on his cheek. 'Later,' she said, 'Okay? I'll put Jack up.'

Desmond was left alone at the sink. He didn't know why he had said that really, about Mark. If he thought he had so much as touched her he'd kill him, he'd frighten the hell out of him if Boyle would co-operate. Jesus, for once the washing-up could wait! He left the kitchen and went into the hall. Aimee was carrying Jack up the stairs.

'It's a pong,' said Jack over his mother's shoulder, trying out the word, 'What a pong!'

'Tell Mummy I'm coming,' said Desmond, 'Tell Mummy to run, Jack, I'm after her!'

'Desmond, do be sensible. What an absolute stink! What is it?'

'Smells like after-shave,' said Desmond. 'Perhaps Boyle's been tarting himself up, practising for tomorrow night.'

'Where is he anyway?' she asked.

'In his room I think.'

Aimee took Jack to the bathroom. Desmond looked out of the window and down to the lake. He went into their room opposite the nursery and stood in profile pulling his stomach in, looking in the mirror, then went across to Boyle's room. The door, he could hardly believe it, was locked.

'You won't believe this,' he said, going into the bathroom. 'He's locked his door again!'

'You're joking.'

'He has, I tell you.'

'Is he in there?'

'Uncle's on his bike, on a cycle ride,' announced Jack, 'without his shoes!'

'Is he, Jack?'

'I saw him.'

Desmond raised his eyebrows at his wife.

'He moved his chest of drawers this afternoon, you

know,' said Aimee.

'Did he? What on earth for?'

'I suppose he wanted his things.'

'It's easy enough to go down to Jack's room, surely?'

'You'd think so. Can't you smell something darling? Open the window.'

'What a pong,' said Jack, self-righteously, 'ugh!'

Desmond opened the window. 'That'll get rid of it,' he said.

'I don't know, I think it's on the landing,' said Aimee, keen to trace it to its source.

Desmond followed her out to the landing, 'Pooh! Look at this!' she said, gazing in disbelief at the runner she had brought to brighten up the floor, 'It's all sticky!'

'Where? I can't see it.'

'There.' She touched it gingerly with her fingers, 'Ugh!'

'What is it?'

She smelt it on the tip of her red nail, 'Shaving cream I think. Honestly, what a mess!'

'What on earth has he been up to now,' said Desmond, thinking out loud, 'Perhaps he cut himself?'

'You don't put shaving cream on a cut.'

'Oh come on, Aimee. Let's go to bed, come on. When you've got Jack down?'

'I'm sorry. I've got to clean this lot up. Look! It's everywhere.'

'Leave it Aimee, walk round it.'

She turned on him. 'Walk round it! That's typical of you. Walk round it! I tell you,' she said, breaking away from him completely. 'I'm just about fed up with your brother and his funny little ways,' she said, flouncing down the staircase. 'I've had enough. You can tell him so from me! Come to that,' she said, turning, looking up, 'I'll tell him so myself!'

'What about Jack?' wailed Desmond.

'You put him to bed for once!'

'Come up and kiss me mummy,' called Jack.

'I'll be up when I've got this cleared and not until!'

'What has uncle done?' asked Jack, as Desmond dried

him.

'Nothing, darling, come on. Beddie Byes.'

'Why is Mummy cross?'

'It's the heat.'

'Why does the heat make her cross?' he asked, as Desmond struggled to get his badly dried body into his pyjamas.

'Do you want a story? Come on, I'll read a story. There's a good boy, leave Mummy alone, she'll cool down in a minute.'

'Will she come and kiss me?'

'I'm hoping she'll come and kiss me.'

'Read this, Daddy.'

Desmond read: 'There was once a dormouse who lived in a bed of delphiniums (blue) and geraniums (red), and all of the day long he'd a wonderful view of geraniums (red) and delphiniums (blue).'

It was a very long poem and when he finally reached the end of it, Jack automatically said, 'Again!'

'Not tonight! That's enough for tonight.'

'Daddy?' asked Jack, stalling, keeping his father in the room.

'What?'

'Why don't grown ups like each other?'

'They do.'

'Mummy doesn't.'

'Don't be silly.'

'She doesn't like Uncle Boyle!'

'Oh she does,' said Desmond. 'She doesn't like him making a mess, that's all. Like when you make a mess. She gets cross.'

'Why?'

'Because she has to clear it up, twit! Now sleep.'

'And no one likes Mark,' said Jack as a final blow, allowing Desmond to tuck him up.

'They do, everybody does, we all like him.'

'Will you send Mummy up?'

'I will.'

'Promise?'

'Promise. Goodnight then,' he kissed his son and the little bare arms came up around his neck. They had forgotten to wash him in the bath but that wasn't the sort of thing that little boys worried about. 'I love you very, very much,' said Jack, spacing out the 'verys'.

'Thank you and I love you. Now go to sleep!'

Desmond left the child's room, wet marks on the runner showed where Aimee had done her scrubbing. He felt he had told more than one person during that long day to go to bed, he only wished he could persuade his wife.

Part Three

Boyle cycled the road to the island as if pursued. A light, early evening breeze made play with the trees and freshened the air that had hung all day, seemingly immovable. He pedalled furiously along, bare feet, bare back, pedalling faster and still faster, a moth to a flame, not thinking of the action of the wheels but just getting there, making the distance.

Boyle was drawn to the island rather in the way that a Christian, but not a church-goer, will sit for a while in some cathedral, absorb the atmosphere and feel strengthened by the experience. It was his enchanted place and like the Happy Isles of Irish mythology it had a timelessness for him, here memories retained their bloom unsullied and unspoilt. This place of broken trees and trailing ivy, broken stones and sponge-thick moss was a place of love remembered. His mother had brought him here as a child. He'd been alone with Desmond here, through the lucky accident of English school holidays which didn't coincide, alone to play with Desmond before Desmond could go off, desert him for someone better, someone else. Later on, moving with the gang, they had come out here on bikes, come to sit and chew the fat on the rusty post and rail fence that enclosed the toothy-blank remains of the Caldragh grave stones and contained the ancient Janus figure. Sat about on scented summer nights swopping boasts and skimming stones until, pestered by the gnats, to clamber out along the shore. It was the place he had hoped to share with Sean.

But there was more to it than that. At its centre stood the stone, double-faced, inscrutable, ancient, unforgiving and strong, the recipient of Boyle's unspoken confidences, the bond between them invulnerable unless one should betray the other. For Boyle it brought together terror, love and subjugation, pulled them taut, hardened to a fist. How this feeling had developed, or whether it had developed at all, whether perhaps it had just existed in its entirety since his first sight of it as a child, he had no idea. Like his father it had always held him and like his father he would always come.

It was a strange journey out because time for Boyle had simply flown away. He'd had his share of worries about time. Anxiety at the thought that he failed to fill it properly, panic that it was going by too fast, desperation that it dragged, sluggish, hardly moved at all, but now as he rode, all of that, badgering time, was suspended, he moved through it, it couldn't touch him now.

The ease with which he had hung through the window from his hell-hole of a room and just said, 'No tea thanks,' became for him a corner stone from which he might now build so that added to his sense of 'no-time' was another one of freedom. He felt free, released, as if in that gesture, that leaning out, the mundane declining of a cup of tea! – he had somehow become unhooked, unshackled. He'd wanted this freedom for ages, he knew that now, he didn't want what they suggested be it tea or anything else, he had thought he ought to want it, he had been a fool! He was glad of the freedom, he accepted it but he was not elated, not thrilled. His face was wiped of emotion as he moved forward, always forward, turning left and right, free-wheeling down the hills going through the countryside all so utterly familiar the landscape that he formed a part of, knowing with regret that he was now free of it too.

Billy Ferguson waved at him. Settling his father's herd back into the field after the evening milking he raised his hand to him as he passed, said something about the breeze, but it didn't register. Boyle cycling on was truly the man of the moment, the present moment. His feet on the pedals and his hands on the chromium handlebars were at last the space he sought between past and future. That was it, nothing more or less. Nothing special or highflying, a breakthrough that no one else would notice, but it was important for him, oh God so it was, it marked the departure from a kind of life that had been a kind of death.

'What I want is nothing,' he repeated this phrase or forms of it until it became a kind of chant, 'nothing' as he pedalled, 'nothing, nothing'. He was the dragonfly now.

He left his bicycle at the top of the small white track and walked down, chewing at a stem of grass. He walked over the plank that crossed the mud, for the cows walk here, come down to the shore to drink, down to where the vegetation is always rather rank because of its position so near to the lake. The grass was wet, the August evening pulling in, he climbed the railings and put the clappers down for Desmond, somewhere hidden but somewhere he might find them easily the following night. Careful not to look at the stone he retraced his steps, climbed back over the railings and went down to the shore, clambered out along the rocks. The lake before him was black, its surface slightly scattered by the little wind, he sat on the wet stones looking out. For once he was able to think with great clarity, unhampered by doubts, misgivings, regret, anxiety, anticipation, guilt or need. The world did not seem plural to him now, it fell as if sliced into neat and equal pieces, slices of black and of white. He thought about this quietly, he marvelled at it, believed it to be true.

He left the shore, padded back across the ground which is largely moss, thick with closing flowers, broken branches that trail with ivy, stones and boulders, back across the very patch where Aimee and the family rug with its chewed-up tassels, had been so casually laid. He buttoned his shirt as he walked, right up to the neck, tucked it into his trousers, secured the cuffs, combed his hair with his fingers, up and away from his forehead. He walked towards the stone and at last he was close enough to touch it. It reached to his thigh bone and he closed his eyes, utterly relieved as he felt it, so familiar, warm from the sun. With steady fingers he felt and rejoiced in those well known incised lines touching first the belt which ran on all four sides of the stone. He outlined each pair of staring eyes, felt for the long spatulate nose and down and across to the upward curling moustache, the hard inside of the down-turned mouth with the suspicion of the protruding tongue, onto the sharply pointed chin, kneeling he felt the phallus on one side. Lovingly he caressed the stone, graciously it calmed him. His hands finally came to rest in the shallow indentation between the twin heads, the libation stoop, the place of offering, empty and dry . . . nothing and again nothing. Impulsively he wrapped his arms right around the old figure and held on very tight his face hard bliss against the warmed, reddish stone.

> 'The dormouse lay happy, his eyes were so tight
> He could see no chrysanthemums, yellow or white,
> And all that he felt at the back of his head
> Were delphiniums blue and geraniums red.'

He took it a lot slower on the way home. It was cooler now and he cycled against the breeze, he took his time, no hurry or rush now and not much worry either. His world had closed in, its possibilities narrowed to a simple 'V', he felt very little except relief. His sweat, drying, had chilled him and he made a last spurt towards the gates, sped through them, forcing them, letting them squeal and grate noisily to an uneven shut. Up the drive and straight round to the front of the house, throwing his bike, leaving it there, abandoning everything.

He could see them through the sitting room window. Desmond beneath the standard lamp writing, Aimee on her knees cutting out a piece of cloth, Dada puzzling behind the latest copy of *The Impartial Reporter* in what must have been virtual darkness; the old enigma of lighted windows, a glimpse of the world within.

Exhausted he trailed in through the darkening hall, pulled himself up the stairs and dressed as he was, dirty, grass sticking to him, black bare feet he fell into bed beside the sleeping Jack.

Aimee discovered the horror coming up to cover up her son. Without fuss, without words she pulled him by the hair, a hand across his mouth until he was out of the bed, beside her. With the coldness of a knife her hand in the small of his stooping back, she propelled him towards the old nursery, felt for the key in his pockets, unlocked it, pushed him inside the door and shut it. Only then did she turn on the landing light. Now muck and grass was on the runner she had cleaned that afternoon . . .

In her son's room she gently pulled the bottom sheet from under him, replaced it with a clean one, wiped the child's face with flannel, snuggled him down again, kissed him. Cold now, in her own room, she found the comfort of her cardigan, which smelt of her, of sense and civilization, of all things known and now with shaking legs she returned to the sitting room.

Desmond looked up, Dada tuned in the wireless for the news. Aimee picked up her paper pattern, folded it into its original creases, her heart bum, bum beneath the cardigan, put her sewing on the dark table beyond the sofa and then, with the scissors in her hands moved until she stood in front of the empty fireplace.

'Desmond,' the cold of the scissors in her hands, the tone of her voice alerting the two men.

'Would you ask your father to turn off the radio?'

'What is it Aimee?'

'Turn it down Dada.'

'Turn it off,' said Aimee through her teeth.

'I've just been upstairs, I've just . . .' and there was almost a giggle in her voice, 'I've just found Boyle in bed with Jack.'

'What's that? What's that you're saying?' Dada stood up his paper slid to the floor.

'Jesus!' said Desmond in broad and panic Fermanagh, 'Jesus!'

Aimee put her hand across her mouth laughter welled up behind it.

'Is he full? Surely to God it's a mistake,' Desmond struggled for some explanation, 'He must be drunk Aimee.'

'Aye,' said Dada, 'and taken the wrong turn. He's been out, that's it. He's not often out. Where is the boy now? I'll go on up. I'll have a word . . .'

'No. I'll have a word. I want to have a word,' she moved the scissors from hand to hand the laughter had quite gone. 'Bastard!' she said, 'Bastard.'

'Now don't be making a fuss, Aimee. It's nothing strange or startling surely, a man comes in full and takes the wrong room. He'll be sleeping it off in his own bed now, isn't that so Desmond? I mind many's the times I'd done the same sort of thing myself, the same mistake like. A man can make a mistake my dear. He'd have had a skinful in the town more than likely, eh Desmond?'

'Sure, we've all done it,' said Desmond and, very much aware of Aimee's need to exact the punishment for the crime added, 'He'll have a head on him like I don't know what in the morning, it'll be as right as rain.'

'What are you talking about Desmond? What are you saying? He's never been "as right as rain" as you put it, you're as bad as he is, you both are. Bastards! He is not okay,' she said slowly now, 'Not okay and never will be. Boyle is disturbed if not right off his head.' She looked at the faces of the two men, hating them, 'And you're both pathetic! Why don't you face it?'

'He's all right!'

'He is not all right.'

Dada turned away from her, 'I'll go up now,' he said

quietly, 'I'll have a word.'

He left the room, Desmond moved instinctively, hopelessly towards the drinks.

'Leave it, Aimee,' he urged, 'I'm sure he was drunk.'

'Very comforting.'

'Give the man a chance.'

'Why should I? No. I won't do that Desmond. I won't. I hate him, I hate Dada, I hate you, I hate this house, I'm going, I'm taking Jack, I'm going in the morning.'

'You're hysterical Aimee, calm down.'

'You're hysterical, you and Dada! You can't see something that's right under your noses. Why doesn't he work Desmond? Why hasn't he ever done anything? Why was he sent away from school? Why does he get letters from young boys in jail? Wouldn't you say there was just something a tiny bit wrong, don't you think? You're keeping it in the family, well, God help me, I'm a member of this family too!'

Desmond took the scissors from her, offered her a drink.

'You drink Desmond, have mine too. It's your solution isn't it. I'm going tomorrow and I'm not coming back, to you, to this, anything.'

Silence filled the room, both wished they were somewhere, anywhere else.

'Did Jack wake up?' asked Desmond eventually.

'Not really.'

'Well then . . .'

'Well bloody what?'

'I think we should forget it.'

Aimee wouldn't even look at him, he went on, 'I'm sure you've got everything a bit out of proportion, honestly. You're letting your imagination run away with you.'

'I never do that.'

That, thought Desmond, was undoubtedly true. The conversation, unresolved, fell into many fragments belonging to other arguments between them which went back a lot further than this.

'I'll make some coffee,' he told her, heading towards the door, 'Come on.'

She burst into tears in the kitchen, he told her as he'd told Boyle, that she was overwrought, blamed, for the lack of anything else that might upset her equilibrium, the weather, the hot weather. Comforting her the playwright in him disliked the role he felt forced to play, telling her that it was all 'okay', soon forgotten, that least said was really soonest mended, reminding her that Dada, who had not been seen since he left the sitting room, was actually an old man now. Aimee observed her husband, she despised him totally.

'Anyway you've got your dinner party tomorrow.'

'I won't be here tomorrow.'

She was crying again. 'Have a good blow,' he said, passing her his hanky. It was covered in feathers.

'Get that thing away from me!'

'Christ!' Desmond threw the hanky in the direction of the bin, tugged at some kitchen paper, handed her a piece. 'Feel better now?' he asked.

'No.'

'Families must stick together,' he told her as they went upstairs. Aimee forbore to comment.

'The mess,' she said as she walked with him towards their bedroom, 'Bastard!'

I hope Dada's all right, Desmond thought undressing, a lot of things said in the heat of the moment, it was, wasn't it, all a mistake? 'The weather's got a lot to answer for,' he said lying down at last, 'I never thought I'd sit in this bedroom and pray for rain.'

Aimee stood looking out of the window, the moonlight showing the curve of the drive, the gates. Mark was under the same moon, her mother . . .

'You told me Ireland was so wet,' she said turning to her husband.

'I did, didn't I. Well, you live and learn you know,' he answered finding another cliché from the store but he was not as confident as he sounded, not as confident now as he pretended to be.

*

The day dawned bright and very clear and continued strongly with none of the portents of storm or breaking that had marked the day before, only the little breeze, blowing from yesterday, picked up the leaves as it passed.

Dada watched the sun come up, picking the detail from the gates, each elongated bill, each tortuous circle, each meandering progress. Aimee watched it and longed, longed for the sun to sink down again and Mark to come, longed for the day to turn into the night.

Dada, barefooted, long gingery hairs on his square big toes, feeling the wet of the dew still upon the grass, walked along the little path he'd made that summer through the burnt out remains of the rhododendrons and out to the edge of the lake. Taking off his robe he stepped carefully out across a line of stones to get his depth and then dived gracefully, scattering the deep brown water, shuddering as he always did with the first shock of the cold for no matter how hot the days were or how many hot days followed one another, the lakes, so vast and deep, could not hold the warmth.

He swam. Crawled vigorously for a few minutes and then turned, warmed up onto his back and drifted in the water, floated looking up at the high blueness of the sky. He had swum more that year than ever before, each night he remembered the shock of the diving cold, becoming more and more obsessed by it. For a man whose life was composed of a series of avoiding actions, this swimming out on the lake, was the perfection of his scheme of things but today the lake seemed nearer to the house, whose troubles now pursued him out and into the water. Personal survival required detachment and he had cultivated it to a fine bloom, he was, what he wanted to be, his own man. 'Never come home until the rest are well in their beds,' should have been his motto, he thought, remembering the horrors of the night before. Desmond had been torn, his favourite son, torn between his wife and his father. Women, were the disintegrating force, and Boyle, an hysterical drunk, not at all! Hysterical but not drunk and Dada had hit him, twice.

He turned over in the water and swam again although it was his usual practice to just float like this for minutes at a time, thinking, dreaming, scheming a little. Today he swam swiftly, rhythmically, strongly thrusting at the water, swimming well but without pleasure to outpace the memory of those heavy swipes.

Desmond had not yet seen the sun and lay slug-like across the crumpled double bed, lay on, even more unwilling than usual to start the day. To wrap up the freckled, sagging body, breathe in as he did the waist button of his jeans, struggle again to make his sandy hair spread, if not luxuriantly, then as naturally as possible around his head. Last night he had made love to Aimee proficiently and with good intentions. Under the circumstances they had both performed well but, like all acts of charity, it had left them cold. It was finished, but not all over, their bodies took the cue. She wouldn't go today, nor tomorrow, in life, he remembered thinking of plays, there's a lot more to it than the slamming of the door. What did the future hold now, what did he want, for he and Aimee had slid now to a temporary full stop. What would they settle for, a new beginning together or apart, or most probably just go on and on, a parallel path paved by pieces of nostalgia, familiarity and cowardice, a path built for little Jack.

Shit! Desmond lit a cigarette finding it often preferable to take the first one lying down. With an effort he turned his thoughts away from Aimee and Boyle and Ballyross to London, work, whatever happened he had resources, he had ideas. Just at the moment, as he now couldn't get out of bed so he couldn't rise to the challenge or even thought of this other world, the real world he thought it, the world beyond the gates. He would of course come round. Like his father he needed women, he enjoyed the chase and saw no reason to stop running. Like drink it brought him out of himself, made him loquacious, charming, a mild drug, like fags, a habit in his thirties he had discovered he couldn't do without. He'd fancied that girl who played Frances in his play, he fancied her more because she'd spurned him. In with a chance there, he thought, probably worth the effort. So: life, from his supine position on the bed, was still worth it he considered, the ash falling from his cigarette to be captured in the fine red hairs on his belly. Fuck Ivan if he didn't use the film, Desmond had other fish to fry. Life was all right on balance and he, Desmond was in control, he thought and then panicked slightly at the thought that it might be Boyle, Boyle that upset the balance, sent life flying. Home ground wasn't safe for Desmond, there was little doubt of that now, he'd stayed too long already. Boyle, Ivan and the film, the Irish connection was best buried, best forgotten every way around.

The day reached him through the windows or he might have lain quite happily like that all morning. The sound of a tractor outside, Mrs Devlin banging out mats, the Hoover presumably choked up on a diet of bird feathers, shaving cream and grass. Jack told to get out of the way was being moved from pillar to post and back again in a flurry of feminine enthusiasm to get things 'just right'. Desmond peered out of the window as he dressed. Aimee had recovered somewhat her face grim with purpose, a scarf covering her hair as if the flick of a duster and the arrangement of flowers was akin to coal mining and required protective clothing. Aimee was back in the driving seat in control.

Boyle hiding in his room, awaiting Desmond's step, emerged from the holocaust of scrumpled, sodden papers not yet discovered.

'Ah Boyle,' said Desmond embarrassed.

Boyle saw Aimee from the crook of the staircase, Aimee ignored him, looked past him at her husband, 'I can't do breakfast now you know,' she said looking at her wrist forgetting she had taken off her watch.

'Move yourself young fellow,' said Mrs Devlin a most unattractive early morning sight, shooing Jack away from her dustpan which he had emptied and was sifting through in his continuing quest to find the tyres from his toy tractor.

'For goodness sake, take him off my hands,' begged

Aimee, 'I must get on.'

'Fine, Fine, just let me get some breakfast okay?' Desmond moved towards the comparative calm of the kitchen.

Boyle followed him in, 'I've got it all fixed,' he said to his brother, 'set up and ready to roll.'

'What?'

'Everything's ready.'

'What's ready?' said Desmond opening the fridge. 'Where's the bacon? Were you drunk last night? There was the most terrible row. Aimee's furious.' Desmond put the pan on the range, 'How's your head this morning?'

'My head's fine.'

'Do you want some breakfast?'

'I do. I'll help. Let's have the lot.' He found sausages, tomatoes, potato bread, bacon, eggs.

'Where did you go last night?'

'Out to the island with the clappers. I hid them in the grass there. It's all set up like I said, like you asked me.'

'You didn't go to the pub then?'

'No.'

Boyle sliced the tomatoes with a loud, owl yell. Desmond recoiled in shock. 'What on earth?'

'Just practising my blood curdling cries for tonight. You know, eeeeh!'

'Don't.'

'Eeeeeeh!'

'Keep your voice down, Boyle, Aimee'll hear you.'

'You didn't tell her then?'

'I'm not crazy!'

'No,' agreed Boyle. 'She wouldn't understand.'

'She wouldn't be amused that's for certain. She hasn't got a sense of humour,' said Desmond and realised as he said so, what it was he had said. It was quite liberating really, small but liberating.

Desmond kept an eye on Boyle, watched him tuck into his breakfast. He was perfectly all right, it had obviously all been a mistake. He rang Ivan who told him that the film was now going ahead and that fees were being sorted out. Did Desmond want him to send the first instalment over to Ballyross?

'No. I'm coming back.'

'Had enough?'

'I can't afford holidays like some people.'

'Give me a call when you get back then.'

'I will, before the weekend.'

'Desmond, I wish you wouldn't follow me about,' Aimee said a little later. She had cleared the kitchen table and was chopping small amounts of various vegetables.

'What are you making anyway?'

'Curry.'

'Curry? Isn't that a bit, I mean, isn't it a bit hot for curry?'

'I don't think so.'

'Couldn't we have a joint or something?'

'Mind out of the way, Desmond. Come on, shift yourself.'

Desmond scooped a piece of tomato off the board. 'I don't think I even like curry,' he said.

'Desmond, please!' said Aimee as she chopped a stalk of celery, 'Leave it!'

'But why do we have to have curry,' he persisted retreating to the dresser leaving her room to chop.

'Mark loves it. It's his favourite dish.'

Desmond picked up the paper and read: 'New wonder drug. People for Peace, Mrs Mairead Corrigan, the aunt of the three children killed on August 10th appealed to the people of the North to come out and show the world they wanted peace. About 20,000 people attended a peace rally in Ormeau Park, Belfast. New confidence to devise forms for living in peaceful, creative relationships with . . .'

The sound of Jack giggling and running wild in the hall came through the open kitchen door. 'Uncle No!' he shrieked.

'Woosh,' came the sound of Boyle's voice, 'Woosh, woosh!'

'Let me, Let me, please me, me!'

Jack screamed with frightened delight. Aimee stopped chopping, 'What is going on out there?'

'Rah, rah, rah!' screamed Boyle, 'Rah! Rah!' came Jack's little voice in imitation and the sound of feet running on the stairs and along the landing.

'Go and see what they're up to will you, Desmond. I can't concentrate with all that going on.'

Desmond put down the paper, Mr Merlyn Rees, the Northern Ireland Secretary, said that he had a high personal regard for Brian Faulkner and that the people of Northern Ireland have cause to be very grateful . . .'

All was pandemonium in the hall. Jack on the stairs waved a long bamboo cane, Boyle a few steps below pranced, danced, waved a sabre sword.

'Christ Boyle! What are you doing?'

'I'm practising my woosh!' said Boyle seriously, turning round and clearing the sword just free of his brother's head.

Desmond leapt quickly out of the way putting his hands to his chest in an automatic gesture of self-defence. Boyle came down the stairs, waving his sword wildly in the air.

'Jesus, Boyle are you crazy? Give it here.'

But Boyle ran up the staircase away from him, 'Woosh! Woosh!'

Jack shrieked with laughter, 'On guard,' he called, 'Touché!'

'Come on Boyle. That's really dangerous. Put it down.'

'It's only a game, Desmond. He loves it,' and it was true, Jack was in delight, ecstasy.

Aimee appeared wiping the juice from the vegetables on her little apron. 'Oh God,' she said, 'Boyle give that here at once you maniac. It's not a real one is it?' she asked her husband.

'Of course it's real, woman!'

'Come on Boyle,' said Aimee as if addressing Jack. 'I'd rather you didn't wave that in here. Come on,' she said briskly, 'You could kill someone.'

But Boyle was well out of reach, wooshing on the landing.

'For goodness sake be careful,' said Desmond.

Boyle put the sword to his side and stood to attention, 'I'm being careful. It's just a game.'

'Come down to mummy, Jack,' said Aimee in her clipped voice, 'Down the stairs now, come on!'

'Won't!'

'Jack!'

'Meanie, meanie!' he called.

'Meanie!' said Boyle and giggled.

'Desmond this is ridiculous,' said Aimee.

'I'm not going to let him have it, Aimee,' said Boyle, 'We're playing, he's got the stick.'

'I don't care. It's not on. Come here Jack, at once, come on. Down here!'

'I want to play!'

'Do as I say!'

'Why?'

'Just do as I say!'

Jack came down the stairs in high dudgeon and went through the sitting room door where his mother directed him, raising his little blonde eyebrows at his uncle. Aimee, victorious, returned to the kitchen. Desmond composed his face to look as if he had never been at all frightened, 'Where did you get it?' he asked.

'It's a sabre. I had it in my room. You know, the Enniskillen Dragoons.'

'No?'

Boyle sang:

They were all dressed up the like of gentlemen's sons
With their bright shining sabres and their carbine guns,
Their brass mounted pistols she noted them too
All because she loved an Enniskilling Dragoon!'

'Where did it come from? I've never seen it before.'

'Dunno,' said Boyle, 'Not very shiny is it? Do you think I should clean it?'

'You could,' Desmond took it from him, 'It's rather nice, isn't it?'

How could he clean it he shouted through to Aimee in the kitchen and walked down there wielding the sword, his brother behind him. He hoped Aimee would notice that he had the sword, Boyle couldn't get the better of him for long!'

Aimee continued to chop. She held a tiny, sharp, serrated all-purpose kitchen knife. 'I don't want to have anything to do with it,' she said but looked at it all the same, drawn to it. 'I hate swords!'

'But this is beautiful,' said Desmond, 'It's very old.'

'I don't care how old it is,' Aimee turned away, 'It's dangerous.'

'It's sharp,' said Boyle.

Desmond ran a finger down it. 'Ugh!' he shuddered, 'it is!'

'Please get out of here! I'm trying to get on.'

The brothers took the sword out into the sunshine and sat on the step. 'Mustn't get under her feet,' said Desmond under his breath.

'I could cut off her feet with this,' said Boyle holding the sabre once more although Desmond could not recall handing it back.

'Ugh!' said Desmond again, 'Still it would be nice to clean it up. Better put it well out of Jack's way, he could really do himself some damage.'

'I will of course. I never intended him to have it, honestly. It was just a game.'

'I know,' Desmond saw that his brother's eyes behind the glasses had suddenly filled with tears; embarrassed he looked away.

'Do you think it's killed anyone?' he asked rapidly changing course. 'It's sharp enough.'

Desmond got out his cigarettes and handed one to Boyle. 'It must have been awful, mustn't it, you know, fighting with swords, bayonets.'

'Close combat.'

'Cold steel. It makes me shudder! Much worse than guns really, aren't they? I mean at least there's some distance.'

'You know what they're saying about Crawford Ferguson?'

'No.'

'The first shot killed him. Then they gave him five more at close range, blew off the top of his head.'

'Jesus!'

'That's what they say,' said Boyle fingering the sword.

'Don't,' said Desmond. 'I'd put it away if I were you, go on. Do it now. I'll see if I can rustle up some coffee.'

Boyle took the sabre upstairs, stood for a moment in the doorway and then flicking the counterpane from the second bed he put it down the bed and then pulled the counterpane straight again. That was a prank too, an apple pie bed.

Jack had escaped from Mrs Devlin and was outside with his bamboo cane, chasing the red cat who was trying unsuccessfully to sleep in the shade of the watering can. Boyle watched him from the step polishing his glasses.

'Only "Instant" I'm afraid,' said Desmond coming out with two mugs and a glass of orange, 'Really you'd think she was expecting the bloody Pope. Why do women fuss so?'

'Search me,' replied Boyle and again Desmond noticed tears behind the glasses and thought to himself, I'm being crass. Boyle doesn't know anything about women. What did I say that for? Tread carefully. 'Have you ever been to the Tower of London?' he asked on a tangent as the thought came to him.

'You know I haven't.'

'You ought to go sometime, really. They've got quite an arsenal. I'm going to take Jack when I have the chance. They have a whole vast hall, just crammed with weapons. Armour, guns, swords, cannon. It's horrible really but fascinating. They've even got children's armour.'

'To fit me?' asked Jack, who was dipping his biscuit into his orange juice and making it all crumby.

'A bit older than you.'

'Extraordinary, the sons of knights all kitted out in this

custom made stuff so that they could practise fighting.'

'I suppose that's reasonable enough.'

'I don't like it though, do you?' said Desmond, 'the idea of children with weapons?'

'We played with guns,' said Boyle, his eyes filling again. 'Everybody does it, Jack does it. It's quite natural.'

'That's not natural, that's imitation.'

'Well.'

'You think it's natural?'

'I do.'

Desmond shook the image from his head.

'Sure half the people fighting in this country are children,' protested Boyle, 'kids, wee cubs. They're always being picked up, thirteen, even younger.'

'Not with guns!'

'With guns certainly! They're all at it, rioting, making petrol bombs, hurling stones.'

'I never thought of that.'

'Perhaps you should.'

'That boy, that friend of yours,' Desmond drank his coffee, 'the one that got picked up, what age was he?'

'Seventeen.'

'A good friend of yours then?'

'Yes.'

Desmond dared not look at his brother, 'I do remember at the beginning,' he said, 'soldiers of the same age being killed. They put the age up, didn't they, eighteen?' Boyle did not reply and he went on, 'It doesn't bear thinking about does it? Kids of that age . . .' Desmond was working himself up into a state now, felt he had to go on talking, 'I mean especially in weather like this, in a place like this. Do you think . . .' he paused and then, 'Go on Jack, run off and play, I want to talk to Boyle.'

'I want to listen.'

'Look,' he handed Jack the empty mugs, 'Go and ask Mummy, very nicely, if we can have some more coffee.'

'But . . .'

'Go on,' he tapped him lightly on the bottom, 'Just ask

nicely.'

'Okay,' said Jack reluctantly, 'Okay. Woosh!' he said as he took the mugs, 'Woosh, woosh, rah, rah!'

'Do you think,' continued Desmond when his son had wooshed out of earshot, 'Do you think it's all right having Mark here?' It had been on his mind for some time.

'In what way?'

'Well, you'll probably think I'm an idiot, but is it safe?'

'What's safe?'

'It couldn't be seen as, sort of, well you know, fraternizing?'

'Seen by whom?'

'Well I mean people must know. You know what this place is like. Everybody knows about everything, you can't sneeze in this county!'

Boyle accepted another cigarette and struck the match on the stoop of the door, Desmond waited impatiently for him to speak. 'I would think,' said Boyle eventually, 'That it was really more dangerous for him than it is for us.'

'How do you mean?'

'Well, if people, certain people, I don't know, knew, that he was coming here frequently, that for instance he was coming here tonight. He could be an easy target. Someone could bump him off.'

Desmond shuddered. 'Who?' he asked.

'I don't know who. It's just a theory.'

Jack called from the hall, 'Daddy, I'm spilling!'

'Hold on. I'll do it,' together they brought what was left of the coffee outside. 'Will we sit under the tree?' he suggested, 'It's more shady.'

'I'm all right here,' said Boyle, sitting up in the direct sun.

'Okay.'

'Is the bird still under there?' asked Jack, poking the hard ground of the flower bed with his bamboo stick.

'Leave it alone, there's a good fellow,' said Boyle.

'It could be gone to heaven,' said Jack in his most trying way, still poking at the earth.

'Leave it,' said Boyle.

'I'll take that stick, Jack,' warned his father.

'It's a sabre!' protested Jack.

'Okay. Take your sabre. Go on. Go off and play. Chase the cat, fight the weeds, someone needs to . . . But has it happened before?' continued Desmond, as Jack disappeared round the side of the house, 'Soldiers, one-off jobs, murdered off duty?'

'Of course it has. That's why he's so glad to come out here. They can't drink in bars, nothing like, take prostitutes, have girl friends, nothing's safe. But he's allowed out here.'

'But if it's so risky for him to come why does he keep coming?'

'Ah,' said Boyle.

'What do you mean, ah?'

'I don't mean anything.'

'You think he's after Aimee, don't you? I'm not completely stupid. That's the quarrel, isn't it?'

'What quarrel?'

'Between you and Aimee.'

Boyle did not reply.

'You think he's after her?'

'I didn't say that.'

'He hardly comes to talk to us!' Boyle still refused to answer. 'I'd kill him if he laid a finger on her,' said Desmond.

'Would you?'

'No. Well, of course not. I'd tell him where to get off though. You don't really think . . .' Desmond failed to complete the sentence.

'It's not my business,' said Boyle.

'I'd kill him if he touched her,' said Desmond, 'break his arrogant little neck.'

'Fighting talk.' Boyle was the older brother this morning, the seesaw rose and fell.

'Well,' Desmond put his head in his hands. Aimee's got no sense of humour, he thought, absolutely none at all.

'Oh, I don't know,' he said lamely, wondering if he was getting yet another headache.

'Don't think about it,' said Boyle.

But Desmond did think about it, 'We'll sort him out tonight, though, won't we,' he said.

'If you like.'

'That'll be a laugh?'

'Yes.'

Desmond stubbed his cigarette out on the gravel. 'Now where's Jack?' he said and called him. 'Jack. Where's he gone now, you have to watch his every move!'

They both got up, 'Jack!' Boyle wandered round the side of the house, no Jack. Jack had disappeared. Jack. He felt suddenly anxious, 'He's not round here,' he said.

'Did he go down to the lake?'

'I don't think so.'

'You go down there. I'll go down by the drive, he's probably half-way up those blasted gates by now. Oh he is wild, I told him not to go off!'

Boyle ran down the length of the garden calling for the boy. His heart raced, tiny Jack, wee cub, he wouldn't harm a hair of the child's head. 'Jack,' he called, 'Jack, Jack!' He met up with Desmond. Have you seen him? No, don't panic said their eyes, keep calm.

Together they ran back up to the house, Boyle went into the sitting room thinking he might be hiding, then upstairs to his room but the door remained securely locked, the sabre safe down the bed clothes of the second bed. Desmond went down the corridor to the kitchen which smelt of onions.

'Seen Jack?' he asked his wife.

'I thought you were looking after him?'

'We were. He just went off.'

'Oh, for God's sake,' said Aimee, 'I can't stand much more of this. Have you looked . . .'

'We've looked everywhere.'

'Mrs Devlin, have you seen Jack?'

'I have not.'

So all four of them now went back out and into the sunlight. 'Jack!' they called. 'Jack! Jack!' Boyle ran across the well field, his legs were made of nightmare lead and the long grass snagged at his trousers impeding his progress. His heart raced and made his calling weak and breathless. Desmond pounded out along the road intimations of disaster that had presaged since his arrival in Ireland came to him in waves of shock. Jack's body floating in the lake, the water in his hair, Jack trampled by cattle, Jack run over, Jack cut to pieces by the sabre. Mrs Devlin checked the house as if she might just, in a fit of over-zealous housekeeping, have tidied him away. Aimee clutched her apron at first unable to move, overcome by hideous guilt. This is my fault, she thought. I shouldn't have done it, I mustn't, God help me!

Boyle found him in a small copse where Dada was fencing. Jack with a stone as a hammer banging in his bamboo sword. He rushed at the boy and held him in his arms. 'Thank God,' he said. 'Found him,' he called breathlessly, 'Found him!' Aimee came, then Desmond. 'Never do that again!' she warned, pulling him away from Boyle, she slapped his bare legs, 'Don't you ever, ever run off like that again.'

Jack fought back the tears. 'I didn't, Mummy! I went with Grampa!'

Aimee turned on her father-in-law. 'You should know better. How can you take him off without telling us. I was imagining all sorts of things!'

'Unusual for you,' said Dada.

Relief flooded them all as they took him back to the house. Aimee scolded, Desmond reproached, Boyle explained. 'It's very dangerous to run off,' they told the little boy. 'You must stay where we know you are. Dada should have told us. You must be more careful. Never go off on your own. You're not big enough yet. Never go near the lake. Tell Grampa you must come and ask Daddy first. You naughty, naughty little boy!'

'Oh God, the onions!' screeched Aimee as they arrived

back at the house and flew into the kitchen. 'I can't stand it. They'll be burnt to a cinder!'

'Now stay with me,' said Desmond. 'I'll walk you down to the gate.'

Mrs Devlin had saved the onions, 'I took them off for you,' she told Aimee, 'There now, on the side.'

'Oh, thank you, thank you Mrs Devlin. You're a real treasure!' She kissed the moley face impulsively, 'I couldn't bear it if this was spoilt.'

'Ach now, Mrs Hamilton, sure you're all wired up. Would you take a wee glass of something, you've had a queer shock.'

'Do you think I should?'

'I'll get you a wee tot.'

Mrs Devlin brought in the whisky bottle that had been much depleted by several days of purely medicinal drinking. 'Here you are now, go on, get that down you,' she put the glass into Aimee's small polished, white hands, 'There now.'

Aimee sniffed and drank the whisky, small tears crept out of her mascaraed lids.

'Ach now. Nothing's burnt.'

The little Ferguson child, that poor woman . . .

'I was so frightened, just for a moment, anything can happen so easily.'

'Ah now, that's it then, that's it surely. They're off like the divil at that age, sure I've had plenty, I know.'

'How many children have you got?' asked Aimee, whose personal contact with Mrs Devlin amounted so far to a mere exchange of dusters.

'I've raised seven.'

'Really?'

'And I've sixteen grandchildren.'

'Good gracious!'

'I'm a lucky woman.'

'You certainly are.'

'Sure I know what it's like,' she said, taking a wee drop herself and pouring a little more into Aimee's glass. 'This place gets you down, it does surely. It wears you thin, this old trouble. That poor wee Betty Ferguson, broken in two pieces!'

'Yes, well . . .'

'And the heat's fierce so it is.'

'It is rather.'

'Would you take a few sandwiches for your dinner?'

'Thank you, that would be lovely Mrs Devlin.'

Aimee sat back and watched Mrs Devlin prepare the sandwiches. Watched her moving back and forth from the refrigerator to the pantry, from the pantry to the meat safe. Watched her butter the loaf first, watched her cut the bread. Oh Jack, Jack! she thought. Darling Jack! Desmond couldn't be trusted, not once he got talking, all talk. Mark, although not on stage, appeared as a rock in this latest drama and the thought that he would soon be there, in a couple of hours, did more for her than the glass of whisky.

'Everything else is done?' she asked.

'It's all done.'

'Good.'

'I'd take a wee rest, if I were you Mrs Hamilton with company coming. I'll come on up later on.'

'Well, I don't think that will be really necessary but thank you all the same. It's very kind of you Mrs Devlin. Thank you.'

I'll give her more money, she thought, a couple of quid. 'You've been very good and thanks for remembering my precious onions!' she said as she walked her to the door.

'Who is it you've got coming then?' asked Mrs Devlin, who knew very well who it was.

'Oh,' instinctively Aimee was careful, 'an old school friend of my husband's.'

'That'll be nice for yous.'

'Yes, well. We've both made an effort.'

'We have surely.'

'Well, thanks again,' Aimee handed over the extra money, accepted the 'God bless yous' graciously and watched the woman cycle off. She sincerely hoped she could get back on a proper footing the next time she saw her. Drinking whisky indeed! Give that type an inch and they took a mile. Come tonight indeed. She'd have to watch her like a hawk over the next few days. Still she had done her job well, she thought, as she wandered back into the chill of the old house. The door knobs shone and each fingerplate gleamed. The sitting room looked quite civilized, all it needed now was a few flowers. She'd take Jack out with her after lunch and pick some, that would be a nice quiet thing for him to do. She lingered a little in the room, pleased with her handiwork, the drama of the morning almost forgotten.

Mark had been invited for seven o'clock and the whole day seemed suspended just waiting for him. Jack had been kept under very close watch since the little episode of the morning, so rigorously played with in the sultry heat that by half past five he was ready to drop. Aimee's excitement clouded her judgment as effectively as alcohol as she sat out in the late afternoon sun streaking her hair with fresh lemon juice in a last ditch effort to look suitably sun-kissed and golden. She had redone her nails with hibiscus pink and looked forward now to painting her rather thin lips with the matching lip wand. Her husband, not in the party mood, had started drinking some time after their sandwich lunch, not a great deal but a little bit here and there to keep the level topped up. He had been reading last week's English paper and, as the rest of the household dressed and casually ran water into the old rolled-top bath tub without regard to water shortages, he delivered an unheeded lecture that they should now really begin to take the drought more seriously and that if the summer continued much longer, lake or no lake, people like them through such wanton acts of selfishness, like washing hair and bathing, would be the cause of long queues at standpipes in the street. As a rather weak protest he didn't wash at all or change the jeans he had so loathingly squeezed into earlier in the day and simply topped them with an old Wrangler shirt that he had discovered in the drawer and no longer did him justice, making him resemble an ageing and overstuffed toy.

Boyle got out the old school tie, the tie, a symbol of Hamilton welcome. Whatever the problem was with Mark it came and went in Boyle's mind in a most irritating and annoying way. He could only catch a glimpse of what it was but this glimpse was enough to remind him of its importance. The whole affair appeared to him that afternoon like a very complicated sum involving three men, five meadows, two steady horses to plough fifteen furrows . . . In any case it was a sum of many parts and as he could not hold the value of each part in his head for long enough he was unable to reach any sort of satisfactory conclusion. He thought perhaps it might be a good idea to get Mark onto paper and with his typewriter balanced on his upturned drawers and sitting on pillows from both beds, he began to write:

I love you, love you, love you. I love you! I'm the dragonfly now, watch me! And I've been there again Sean. I did it and it's all going to be all right. I no longer care – a fig! Christ, I've been a fool but it's never too late. Never say die, eh boy! Too easily defeated, too weak, too easy to push around. I love Jack and I love Desmond, despite it all, everything. He took Dada away from me – you know that – when we were children. He took my confidence then but everything's fine now, dandy. Even with you it was the old black dog. I went into it with the idea of defeat, good old defeat eating into me, wearing me away, old friend. That's all finished, over. I'm both through it and through with it. All the things, everything I ever wanted to say to you, were really just this, that I love you. That. That is the sum total, the addition of it all, simple addition.

Mark is coming, we're all dressed up. Drinkies on the terrace, dinner in the dining room. Our Mrs Devlin, your Auntie B, is enjoying all this enormously, now does her housework with an awesome 'Fuck the Brits!' expression that would put the fear of God into any gunman. She can out guile the Aimees of this world, the Aimees of this world haven't got a fucking clue! Desmond's dithering, doesn't know it but he is. Not at all sure where to put his feet. Not sure which side to come down on or with how much weight, not sure whether to come down at all. Nasty little barbed wire fence for Dessie. He has got Jack, I suppose, but I could have a son of my own. How about that! I could have a son like Jack. My own boy. I could still have a son. They're calling and I must go down, take control of your life, don't let things slip, I love you Sean, please don't forget.

Boyle stopped here, pushed the typewriter onto the floor and fell backwards onto his pillows. Still ignoring their calls he rescued the letter, just a little torn, and folded it, held it in his hand. Straightening the incongruous short tie in the mirror he went downstairs and outside to where the family had assembled on inside chairs placed at a conscious random angle waiting for Mark to arrive on time which of course he did; stepping from his car every inch the decent chap, prompting Desmond to slouch further in his chair.

'Good to see you,' he said, nodded with impressive vagueness.

'Ah, hello there,' said Boyle, standing up.

Mark put out his hand to shake and felt a piece of folded paper in his palm; Boyle apologized for what had come between them and dropped his letter into the flames of pine needles and charcoal which Desmond had made at Aimee's request to keep the gnats at bay.

Dada shook the soldier's hand. 'How do you do, how do you do,' he said, slightly nodding his head, and noticing as he did so the mirror polish on the shoes and double knots of the laces, the crease of the trousers, the cut of the man.

Now Aimee, who had dashed inside at the first sound of the gates, appeared from the house and walked towards the group, her hands extended in greeting. She had planned this most carefully and her forethought paid off. She did indeed look most attractive approaching them, small, tanned and beautiful. Mark's heart leapt a little behind the Van Heusen blue and white. He had always had attractive women, to him it was as important as driving a decent car.

'I say, this is really super,' he said, accepting a chair, one leg of which prodded into the edge of flower bed which contained the much disputed, very dead, tit. They all smiled on cue but Boyle rather overdid it with a manic Cheshire cat of a smile which refused to subside gradually and in the proper way and just suddenly collapsed, his face sad, awful.

Desmond was determined at this moment that he was not going to pull his considerable weight or do anything at all to make the evening a success. Dada too switched off, disappointed that his son would not pick up the gauntlet and fight, and waited for a suitable moment to find an excuse to leave.

'And how's the badminton?' Mark asked his hostess.

'Honestly I haven't had a game for ages, not since you were here. It's hard to get these boys on their feet,' she said. The natives were lazy as well as revolting.

'I gather you're quite a sportsman, sir?' said Mark to Dada.

'Ah.'

'Swimming isn't it?'

'Yes. I swim,' he said, 'I love the water.'

'The lake's quite safe, you'd say?'

'The lake is safe. It is surely. There are one or two wee beaches. There was a fair deal of swimming in the old days, races, galas . . .' his voice tailed off.

'We thought you'd like to come out to the island?' said Boyle leaning forward in his chair and getting Mark in focus.

'I would, indeed.'

'We thought tonight?'

'Sounds wonderful. You should have told me, I'd have brought my togs.'

'Wrong end of the stick,' said Boyle and explained that

they were going out to look at the stone.

Desmond thought of the stick and shuddered, the bamboo cane and Jack, woosh! woosh!

'Very kind of you both. I'm sure another time would do if it's inconvenient?'

Aimee looked as if it was extremely inconvenient sipped primly at her sherry.

'Beautiful on a night like this,' said Dada. 'A whole crowd of us would go, swim right to the raft, there used to be a raft. The summers were a bit like this one but the water in the lake was never warm, you have to strike out, strike out. Not buoyant like sea water, of course no salt in it this far up you see . . .'

'Which island is it?' asked Mark turning the angle of his chair and looking beyond the burnt out remains of the rhododendrons, 'There are hundreds of them!'

'One hundred and seventy,' corrected Desmond at random.

'The Boa Island,' said Boyle, 'You can reach it by road, I cycle out.'

'And I swim out,' said Dada, 'I don't miss a day.'

The conversation was of the dying fall variety reminded Desmond of cultured, artificially created waves made for testing ships, waves that didn't break. Waves wall to wall without space enough to break in.

'This place is so perfect!' Mark said looking away from the decaying house, 'What a setting! I suppose you don't really see it after a while, take it for granted?'

'I have never taken it for granted,' said Dada.

'Northern Ireland is so beautiful,' continued Mark, 'I never realised. I mean I simply had no idea. Why, Fermanagh is just as good as the Lake District.'

'Better,' said Dada.

'Well yes, absolutely. None of those ghastly coach parties. No cream teas! The Lake District can be pretty grisly in the summer,' he admitted like someone whose cream tea had been completely ruined by the sound of an uncultured voice, the sight of an acrylic sweater.

Dada just looked at him, Aimee took the relay baton of

the conversation and raced on. 'Oh you're right,' she said beaming, 'I think it's an awful shame the way places get absolutely spoilt by trippers, it must be simply awful for the people who live there!'

'Grim!' agreed Mark. They both shook their heads.

'That's how they make their money,' said Desmond. 'Tourism is one of England's biggest money spinners.'

'I know darling,' said Aimee, 'but money makes everything so, well, so sort of squalid, I just think it's a real shame, poor Lake District!'

'But they must make money out of these beauty spots,' agreed Mark.

'I understand that, of course. I just think it's a pity that they can't do it in a more, a more tasteful way, attract the right sort of people.' Her mother said that the right sort of people didn't have money any more and probably couldn't afford to go to the Lake District but she resisted the temptation to say this knowing that some of the assembled company wouldn't understand.

'They won't do it here, will they!' asked Mark looking into the empty bottom of his glass as if searching in desperation for a denial of such a dreadful fate.

'I'm sure they'd love to,' said Desmond. 'Fermanagh is a very poor county, nothing but reeds, rushes and bog. I think the lakes should be exploited.' Mark and Aimee looked at him, he was shouting, 'That's what they're for,' he ended, 'after all.'

The conversation plunged. Aimee looked awkwardly at her glass, at Mark. Mark keeping his eyes away from Boyle who was smiling again in a most unnerving way.

'Exploitation,' stumbled Desmond, 'really only means . . .' Desmond gulped at his whisky, 'only means to turn something to account. The Lakes should be turned to account.'

'You mean made money out of?' said Aimee.

'Yes, darling, I do. That's it exactly. An exploit you see,' he said almost to himself, 'is where the word comes from, and an exploit is a brilliant achievement.'

'Choking up the beautiful places with picnickers and coach parties and crisp papers and mobile lavatories is hardly a brilliant achievement.'

'You don't think so.'

'No.'

'Actually . . .' Mark paused and tapped a Benson & Hedges cigarette sharply on the packet and offered them around, 'Boyle, cigarette?'

'I think I will.'

'Good man. Actually,' he started again lighting the cigarettes Desmond dodging rather than take third light. 'Tourism is just one of the areas where Northern Ireland can benefit from Britain's mistakes. A lot of our tourism, roads, motorways, housing is quite up the shoot. Seeing our mistakes you lot should be able to benefit.'

'Because we're so much further behind,' said Dada.

'Exactly,' said Mark, 'Well, the point is that things have moved at a rather slower, you might say more gentlemanly pace, you haven't got the population for a start.'

'Lord don't give us more people, we've enough problems with the ones we've got already,' said Dada, a statement that was followed by rather nervous laughter.

'Mmm well,' said Aimee, 'This is all a bit much for me. I think I'll just go and take a peep at the food.'

'Make sure it doesn't escape,' said Boyle and laughed.

Aimee ignored him and placed her half-empty glass on the crumbling top of the little wall.

'Need any help darling?'

'No. You men chat away.'

But Dada followed her up, 'I've a few beasts to look at . . .'

'Now?' said Aimee, 'We're eating in a quarter of an hour.'

'Time enough,' said Dada.

Left on their own the three men sat silently for a moment watching the fire.

'How about another one?' suggested Desmond and poured more whisky.

Boyle handed his glass but it was still almost full. 'Hey up, you haven't drunk it yet.'

'Oh no,' said Boyle, 'silly me.'

Desmond had the impression that Mark was watching him drink. 'Makes you thirsty,' he said indicating the fire, 'Smoke catches you in your throat.'

'Thanks. I think I will. Tell me a bit about this old stone of yours, Boyle,' he continued leaning towards Boyle earnestly like a teacher intent on bringing out a difficult child, 'I'm intrigued.'

'The Boa stone is a pre-Christian Idol,' said Boyle flatly, automatically. 'It's a janiform figure, double-headed, between the two heads is a libation stoop . . .' he choked and began to cough; Mark leant across to pat him on the back. 'Sorry!' said Boyle. He began to laugh then his laughter belling out in the silence. Mark cleared his own throat in an embarrassed way.

'Share the joke,' commanded Desmond.

'Sorry,' said Boyle still laughing.

'You had this idol on the film you did, I suppose?' asked Mark thinking it best to ignore Boyle.

'Yes,' said Desmond, 'It's an interesting piece. Very, very old. Some of my colleagues,' he was being pompous now and he knew it, 'found it had a sort of presence. It's in a beautiful, rather enigmatic setting and I think that helps of course. I have heard they're thinking of moving it. Safer of course but rather a shame.'

'The filming went well, I gather.'

'Mmm. All on a rather simplistic level of course.' Both knew that they had had almost the exact conversation before but like desperate archaeologists they went over the ground for sherds. 'You know what it's like,' continued Desmond vaguely. Out of the corner of his eye he was watching Boyle whose face was streaked with tears. 'I think this smoke's getting a bit much don't you?' he said.

The smoke was indeed now drifting straight into their eyes, Mark moved his chair a little so that the bulk of his body was now resting on the tit's grave.

'Perhaps we ought to go in,' suggested Desmond still watching his brother. 'Hardly know which is worse,' he said moving Mark along, 'being smoked out or bitten to pieces.'

'Quite,' said Mark.

The house smelt of polish and roses, curry and decades of rising damp. They moved into the sitting room and stood awkwardly turned towards the long windows looking out into the garden.

'I see you're interested in old records,' commented Mark spying a pile of 78s teetering on a bamboo table.

'Not me. My father. Would you like to hear something?'

'Why not.'

Boyle came in and wandered about the room, he looked exhausted but normal, perhaps a little angry. Desmond supposed this was better than the manic grin. He took a record out of its brown paper sleeve with care and put it on:

'You say tomatoe, and I say tomato.
You say potatoe, and I say potato.
Tomato, tomatoe, potato, potatoe,
Let's call the whole thing off!'

'Who is it?' asked Mark.

'Fred Astaire and Ginger Rogers,' replied Desmond with awful resignation.

'Oh yes. Damn good films,' and then, as if to clear up a point, 'I saw them on television.'

'Really,' said Desmond watching Boyle.

'You don't have a goggle box here then?' Mark asked Boyle bringing him into the conversation.

'No,' Boyle shook his head and then continued to shake it in a very noticeable way. Desmond was sure he was doing it deliberately and found it rather amusing. Fuck Mark anyway.

'Oh no, I think you're absolutely right, absolutely,' Mark said, looking hard at the record player, a mono Dansette, with awe and admiration it did not rightly deserve. 'TV ruins conversation.' Boyle was singing, Mark smiled at him indulgently. 'No, as I say,' he said turning his conversation to Desmond, 'TV ruins the old chat but on the other hand one mustn't bury one's head in the sand.'

'Why not?' asked Boyle.

'Well I mean. Don't think for a moment that I watch everything or anything, far from it, don't have time for starters. Still there is a lot to be said for selective viewing,' he looked hopefully at his watch. Aimee had said a quarter of an hour. 'I suppose you have to watch a certain amount for your work?' he asked Desmond, 'but you wouldn't watch much apart from that . . .'

'Oh all the time. Anything and everything, love it, can't get enough! I find it so difficult to understand people who have a thing about television,' he said looking straight at his unfortunate guest, 'as if it offends some moral code. I think it's snobbery you know, people just won't admit to watching it, like masturbation!'

Mark took another cigarette quite aware that he was chain-smoking. 'I said I watched it, just that I choose my programme as one would a good wine. You can't drink just any old rubbish.'

'You may have to tonight,' said Boyle and giggled again, leaving Mark to have a good look at his shoes to see if the polish still glistened.

Aimee appeared like a saving angel, popping her head around the door. 'I think we can eat now. Would you like to come this way?' She smiled prettily at Mark with hibiscus lips, everything about him was wonderful including his shoes. Mark put down his glass. 'No, do bring it through with you,' she said.

The windows were still open in the dining room and the curtains billowed out into the garden. They were to sit grouped at one end of the glistening rosewood table. There were candles on the sideboard and Aimee had found from somewhere a tall trestle affair, the dumb waiter, a vision and word straight from the brothers' collective past. On the table the silver had been cleaned, roses swam in a pair of matching pewter swans.

'What a lovely room,' said Mark.

'I'm glad you like it,' said Aimee, 'It is lovely. Now you sit here, ah Dada, at last. You sit at the head of the table, and Boyle there. Too many men,' she said, 'always a problem.'

'I'm sure Mrs Devlin would have come if you'd asked her,' said Desmond.

'Well, we won't fight over her,' said Mark.

'Now please help yourselves,' she said. Everything that curry involved, popadoms, shredded apple, finger-bowls, bombay duck, dahl she had prepared for him. 'It isn't very hot,' she fussed, 'pickle and chutney. I thought it would be better that way. Now come on, please do help yourself.' Desmond staggering slightly after an extra tot of whisky served himself from the dumb waiter. I married a complete idiot, he thought, boring but beautiful, dumb.

'What's this?' asked Dada picking up a popadom in his large, unaccustomed hand and crushing it in a thousand pieces.

'Oh dear, a popadom,' she said. 'They are a bit crumbly!'

'This is really delicious,' said Mark, wishing he'd never come, like Jack at a birthday party, desperate to go home. 'Curry must be your speciality.'

'I don't think she's ever cooked it before, have you darling?'

'Don't be ridiculous darling! We're always having curry.'

'Are we darling?' 'Darlings' flew in the air like bats.

'You shouldn't have gone to so much trouble just for me,' said Mark melting her so that she laughed and blushed.

'Oh nonsense, you said you liked it.'

'Was your father in India?' asked Dada.

'No sir. I just developed a liking for it. There are quite a few first class Indian restaurants in London.'

'How many?' asked Boyle and Mark looked at him hard to see if he'd heard all right. Either Boyle was drunk or offensive, knowing the Irish, it was probably both. The telephone rang and Aimee put down her fork: 'Oh no! Who on earth could that be?'

'I'll go darling,' said Desmond glad to get away, I'll get another whisky while I'm at it, he thought. He took his glass out with him and picked up the receiver half-heartedly in the hall.

'Isn't it awful the way people ring just as one is about to eat!' exclaimed Aimee quite put out.

'How do they know!' said Mark in the same tone.

'They seem to though, don't they? I wonder if I should put Desmond's in the oven?'

'I should think it would stay hot,' said Boyle and laughed uproariously at his own joke.

The old man picked nervously at the unusual food. Mark slid his hand beneath the table and along Aimee's warm, bare thigh, comforting her, thanking her, exciting himself.

'Well, they're taking their time about it whoever they are,' she said with a laugh in her voice.

In the hall Desmond was talking to Bernie. He'd rung earlier on, left a message. Bernie staying with his mother over in Essex. Essex, it seemed a very long way away. Desmond arranged to meet him in London at the weekend, he'd take him to dinner, do an 'Ivan' on him, soften him up a bit. If Aimee and Desmond were really parting company Desmond would need Bernie, need his London flat for a little longer than the duration of the play.

'You're all right are you?' Bernie questioned, Bernie the good old mate.

'Fine,' lied Desmond, 'see you on Saturday.' Wearily he replaced the receiver, momentarily struck by guilt, went back to the sitting room and drank some whisky from the neck of the decanter, then carried it through with him to the dining room with a sinking, guilty, heart.

'Who was that darling? You were ages.'

'Bernie.'

'Oh? What does he want?'

'Nothing special, nothing.'

Nothing thought Boyle the word echoing in his head, nothing, nothing, nothing.

Aimee and Mark were discussing America, the brothers

sat in silence preoccupied with their own thoughts, half-listening, half-watching the dance.

'I'd adore to go to the States,' said Aimee.

'I think you'd love it actually. Marvellous for a holiday, wouldn't like to live there, bit hectic for me.'

Hectic, Boyle said the word over to himself. He ran through the streets of the city searching for Jack, his voice hollow in the subway, he called from the top of the building, he galloped down the hundred steps towards the street, he pounded the hard pavement, 'Jack! Jack!'

Dada apparently oblivious, got up slowly leaving most of his meal on his plate, 'If you'll excuse me . . .'

'Oh you're not going?'

'One or two things . . .' muttered the old man, 'To see to, you know . . .'

Mark leapt to his feet as if tugged by an invisible, imperative string, 'Very nice to have met you sir,' he said thrusting out his hand.

Dada ignored his hand, turned, walked out.

'Oh dear!' Aimee blushed with embarrassment. 'Don't worry,' she said to her guest, 'It's not you, he gets like that, moody, the Irish are very moody.'

'Is that so?' said Boyle.

'It's sort of melancholy,' she said ignoring him, 'Desmond's got it too, haven't you darling?'

Desmond registered the comment but only just, by now he was seriously drunk.

'I can't imagine where it comes from,' Aimee prattled on.

From a bottle, thought Mark, but didn't say so. Desmond had really been putting it away, especially since the phone call, and Boyle, well he couldn't be far behind.

'Could I have a little more?' said Boyle passing his plate.

'Certainly. You serve yourself.' Her accompanying smile was ice. 'I don't know how you can eat so much in this weather. I peck at my food,' she said addressing her comments to Mark alone, 'this tiny little tummy!' longing to be alone with him, wishing, wishing the brothers would either go to sleep, or go away.'

'I'm keeping up my strength,' said Boyle apparently totally recovered. 'No. Keeping my strength up. That's it! Now where was I, rice.'

Morosely Desmond poured another drink and offered the decanter to Mark who accepted it readily, feeling he had more than earned it. The evening was most awkward, he grabbed at any help he could get. 'I say,' he said, 'Oughtn't we to be going out in this boat?' He winked at Desmond who did not wink back. 'Don't know much about the Celtic world myself. Horned helmets and woad wasn't it? That's about my limit I'm afraid. Oh and Queen Boudicca of course, buried up on Hampstead Heath wasn't she? I love the heath do you know it all?'

'Do you remember the history master?' Desmond cut in, 'D'you remember Mr Percy.'

'Old "wide and far reaching", I do.'

' "Wide and far reaching", that's right,' said Desmond, 'A complete tit!'

'He was, wasn't he, awful old duffer,' Mark felt slightly more at ease, on firmer ground at last.

They talked a little of school, of the history master, of history.

'Revolting peasants,' remembered Desmond.

'Ireland in turmoil,' remembered Mark.

Funny looking back . . .

Aimee began to collect the plates together. When Mark caught her eye, she smiled but the evening was really in ruins, in tatters for her. She hadn't planned it like this, dear God, she'd thought about it enough! Three drunken sots reminiscing about school! Hardly fair, she thought after the work she'd put in. Her lips tightened beneath the professional strokes of hibiscus pink. Men among men were always disappointing, behaved so grossly somehow. Aimee wanted to lead a stately dance, a minuet perhaps, not a rugby hoolie or an Irish jig.

Desmond emptied his glass and clinked it with Mark. 'To the Celts! I suppose,' said Mark. 'The Celts!' said

Desmond, the glasses crashed together again and one broke on the table.

'Oh dear, I am sorry!'

'Watch your fingers!' warned Aimee, 'No, let me.'

Boyle had gone very pale. Desmond's blood fell in tiny droplets on the rosewood table. That was the end then, Aimee fetching a plaster, Aimee holding Desmond's finger under the cold tap.

'Anyway, anyway! To return to the Celts!' insisted Mark when Desmond had returned.

'Here's to them,' said Desmond and emptied his glass again.

'Go easy darling,' said Aimee coldly.

'I'm quite all right, darling. I can take a drink.'

'The Celts!' Mark thumped the table in a most unpleasant school-boy fashion, 'Information gentleman please!'

'Boyle's your man. Don't look at me. He's got woad in his veins.'

Boyle could not be drawn.

'No woad?' asked Desmond generally.

'We want woad!' said Mark.

'Woad, Woad!' repeated Desmond taking up the cry and felt the flap of flesh where the glass had cut his finger.

'Course, I know about the chariots,' said Mark accepting a brandy from Desmond and swilling it round and round in the bowl of the glass.

'What about them?'

'Cuts both ways as Boudicca said reversing!'

'Talk of the devil,' said Desmond recovering from a fit of laughter, catching Aimee by the leg as she re-entered the room. 'To Boudicca our Queen.'

Aimee gave her husband a long, hard, cold look. No one had touched the puddings!

'Shall we go into the other room?' she said.

'We're for the boat,' said Desmond.

'Away three men in a boat.'

'Surely you're not going now?' she said.

'It's now or never,' sang Desmond as Dada might have done.

'But it's dark!'

'The Irish, my darling, are not afraid of the dark.'

'I think you're very silly,' she said deciding to stop it now, smiling at Mark. 'Aren't you a little bit, haven't you had rather too much to drink?'

'I don't think so,' said her husband, 'You don't think so do you Mark, do you Boyle?'

'Go some other time,' urged Aimee. 'There's no point going out now. 'It'll be pitch black by the time you get there.'

'We are going out in a boat,' said Desmond pushing his warm large face near to hers. His breath stank of alcohol.

'And you're coming with us,' said Mark boldly.

'At this hour?'

'Come on darling, darling Aimee,' said Desmond.

Mark got up saying something about gum boots to save his shoes; could Boyle 'Kit him out'? Aimee and Desmond were left alone in the dining room with the remains of the curry, the untouched lemon sorbet, the perfect crème caramel.

'Come on darling!' urged Desmond.

'Not with you in this state.'

'Mark isn't exactly sober.'

'That's different.'

'Oh yes! Why is that different?' he mimicked her clipped little voice. 'Tell me why! I would have thought one drunk was much the same as another.'

'You'd be wrong then.'

'You really fancy him don't you! "Oh Mark hello, have some curry Mark, we have it all the time!" '

'Shut up!'

'Oh Mark,' he mimicked.

'Be quiet!' They'll be back in a minute, they'll hear you.'

'I don't give a monkeys who hears me, it's my house!'

'Boyle's house.'

'All set for off?' Mark appeared in Boyle's jacket and

Dada's boots.

She walked with the three of them to the front door leaving the candles guttering in the dining room.

'We can't persuade you to accompany us?' asked Mark taking advantage of the semi-darkness of the hall to feel for her and squeeze her hand.

'Not tonight.'

The brothers went outside, on impulse she put her arms about his neck standing on tiptoe.

'I wish you'd come,' he said.

'No. Midnight boating's not for me.'

'We'll go out together again, in the afternoon,' he kissed the top of her fingers, 'Aimee!'

'All right.'

'Right. To the Celts,' he said raising his voice and left to join the others. He grabbed Boyle by the arm, 'Come on!' he challenged, 'To the boats!'

'I cycle,' Boyle pulled himself free.

'Come on!

But Desmond was tugging at Mark from the other side, 'The boat's down here,' he said, 'Boyle cycles.'

Time lapsed and lurched for both of them out there on the water, drunken men falling into the boat and from then on all around it.

Desmond sat in the stern hopelessly trying to assess the damage of his drunkenness. Mark sang as he rowed in the semi-darkness, the little boat moving forward in the night. He pulled out strongly and away from the shore as he'd done with Aimee. Now the surface of the lake was just a little bumpy, the night was warm and full of sounds which came to them between the rhythmic splashing of the oars.

'Two men in a boat,' said one of them. 'Women and children first!'

Time slid and tripped so that neither was sure of the pause between a question and an answer. At one moment the journey seemed a long one, at another remarkably short. Although their eyes quickly grew accustomed to the dark, it too changed, as small clouds crossed the moon for seconds at a time. Mark's voice skidded on the lyrics of the songs, 'One man went to row, went to row a boat. One man, one man and his dog, went to row a boat.'

'Less of the dog.'

'He barked.'

'Hair of the dog!'

They giggled.

'One man went to Boa, went to the Boa island.'

Desmond's head was fuzzy, the day coming and going for him in a series of jumbled shots, an editor's nightmare taken through the wrong lens of the camera. What Boyle had said and what Aimee had done. Did he relish being out on the lake with this singing, lord of a man? He could sing, by God he could sing! He trailed his hand in the water then wiped it over his face.

'You're wearing my brother's jacket? My brother's jacket?' he said with effort getting from the beginning of the sentence through, past the middle and to the end.

'One man in another man's jacket went to row a boat.'

'Well, I'll row the boat ashore.'

'Wine, women and song, that's what they promised me,' said Desmond.

He thought lovingly of Aimee and then remembered that she was a bitch.

'Gimmee that jacket!' he said and moved forward suddenly in the boat which rocked alarmingly.

Mark rowed on.

'I said. I said. Gimmee that jacket!' repeated Desmond standing up and advancing towards Mark unsteadily.

'Hey! watch it old man!' Mark held the oars in one hand and pushed Desmond in the stomach. He sat down heavily on the floor of the boat which held a little water.

'Shit!' he exclaimed.

'The person who is rowing is the captain,' said Mark. 'The captain gives the orders!'

Desmond sulked, his bottom wet. 'Keep the jacket!' he muttered. 'Keep it!' and then remembered that it was

Boyle's jacket and Boyle was cycling off to give Mark the shock of his life. That was it. 'The clappers,' he said, triumphant, out loud. 'Go like the clappers!' he yelled in silence.

'I'm doing my best.'

At this moment the bottom of the boat scraped gently on the pebbles.

'Heave ho!' said Mark looking into the gloom. 'This is it, isn't it?' He shipped the oars.

Desmond tried to stand up but promptly fell down again, now his knees were soaking too. 'Hang on, hang on,' he said, 'Hang on,' but the scratching sound faded as the boat floated off again. Pressing his arms hard on the thwart, Desmond tried again and fell again, hitting the side of the boat. Mark put his hand out to steady him and one of the oars slipped from the rowlooks and floated out of reach.

'Jesus, now you've done it!' said Desmond.

'I've done it?' yelled Mark furious, but Desmond was over the side, plunging in the water which came up to his waist.

'Fuck!' he screamed, the cold getting to him, there was something about cold when you'd been drinking. He couldn't remember what it was.

'I'll get it, I'll get it, Captain,' he said tugging his forelock, looking for the oar.

'Grab the painter, for Christ sake!' commanded the Captain.

Desmond struggled in the water, his jeans stuck to his legs.

'Forget the oar, grab the painter!' repeated Mark. They giggled helplessly.

'Boyle, Boyle,' called Desmond, but there was no reply. He continued to giggle, now Mark stepped out into the water and between them they pulled the boat, the oar had floated off and rested gently in the nearby reeds.

They tugged the boat moving with difficulty in their wet clothes.

'All systems go,' said Mark, 'Ssh. Quietly now,' with a

final yank they pulled it right up onto the beach. It jarred on the rough stones beneath.

'Sure you'll wreck the bottom altogether,' warned Desmond but he couldn't help laughing. It was well up now and they both fell, exhausted, on the stones. A cloud crossed the moon.

'Jesus! I can't see a thing,' said Desmond and he felt in his pocket for matches but they were soaking and his hand no longer seemed to fit his pocket.

'Take it,' commanded Mark handing him the painter, 'Run it round that stump.'

'What stump? Oh that stump, that stump,' he did as he was told. 'Ach!' he exclaimed realising that his cigarettes were sodden too.

They lay panting then looking up at the dark sky. Desmond's head spun, like sunbathers they lay waiting for the cloud to cross.

'It's a big one this time,' said Desmond.

'As the actress said to the bishop.'

Desmond began to giggle again, 'Sheee!' he spat out hysterically holding on to his legs, his arms around his sodden jeans, rocking with laughter.

'Where is it?' asked Mark.

'Where is he,' corrected Desmond.

'It. The hip flask.'

'I want the guide,' said Desmond and they began to call him then, 'Boyle, Boylee, Boyleee!'

Desmond could not keep track of what he was meant to remember. He was to lead Mark up to the stone. His body felt like lead. If he could just get that hip flask off him, jammy bastard! Ach, he could sleep, he opened his eyes and the moon went round and round.

'Onward!' commanded Mark.

'Hip flask first,' insisted the mate.

'Where is the flask?' echoed Mark feeling in the borrowed jacket, patting it. 'Still here.' Fumbling with cold fingers he unscrewed the top and took a long, warming, drink.

'Let's have it,' said Desmond. He swung at him and got the flask, a large part of it spilt, wasted on the damp pebbles.

'Give!' said Mark but Desmond was up now.

'Can't catch me,' he whispered giggling, 'Can't catch! Can't catch!'

But Mark was too quick for him, rolled on his side and catching the leg of Desmond's jeans pulled him down, hard, the rocky pebbles came up to meet Desmond as he fell with a thump. He lay dead drunk and feeling no pain.

'Give!' said Mark and opened up Desmond's clenched fist. 'Give!' he commanded. He yanked it from his grasp and took a gulp.

Desmond lay sprawled and made no attempt to move. Mark took a second gulp and thumped his partner on the back.

'Fair is fair,' he thumped. 'I'm the captain and I give the orders. Now,' he took another gulp, 'Now you.'

Desmond did not respond and Mark put the flask down on the ground, 'All right are you?' he asked, 'Are you all right?' He crawled down beside him to get a look at his face and then Desmond sprang, leapt up, grabbed the flask and began to make it up the slope along the stones.

'Can't catch! Can't catch!'

'Shamming bastard,' yelled Mark after him, infuriated at being so easily duped. In a second of bright moonlight he saw Desmond making off into the little wood, then another cloud crossed and he was in darkness again. He was up and half running behind Desmond, when in the darkness, Desmond disappeared.

'Desmond!'

'Can't catch!'

'Can't see let alone catch,' said Mark. 'Old man,' he said, 'Hang on. Hang it all!'

But Desmond was away now on the familiar ground. He walked in the general direction of the stone, made out the post and rail fence, was over that and walking towards the stone and nearly fell on top of it.

'Fuck!' he said resting the flask in its stoop, holding his toe.

'I'm coming,' came Mark's voice.

'Boyle,' whispered Desmond, 'Boyle,' but there was nothing. 'Come on man, it's me, Dessie,' he leant on the stone and then just slouched down beside it. 'Come on,' he said. 'Why is it you can get nothing right,' he said to himself, 'even a fucking joke.' He listened for his brother and then burped loudly. Now the moon appeared again, lit up Mark, half way over the railings.

A wailing sound came above them and a hard flap, flap. In the moonlight Desmond noticed a sheet of black plastic, probably blown there from a silage clamp, flapping nastily in the branches. Then the wailing sound came again.

'Whee,' said Mark letting out his breath.

Desmond giggled. It was Boyle all right and doing his stuff.

The noise came again.

'What is it?' said Mark.

'Banshee,' Desmond giggled and burped loudly.

'Christ,' said Mark. Something far back in his drunkenness, something filed under a different occasion, came into his head. He wasn't in the right place, or the right place at the wrong time? He swayed a little on his feet and the world shifted round. It was all a joke, a silly joke. 'Soldier in Joke,' he thought, 'Not on, not on.' The moment passed and he felt out with his hand and touched the stone now bathed in moonlight. 'This it?' he asked, 'Can't see a damn thing.'

'Pax,' said Desmond and handing him back the flask, 'To the Celts!' he said.

'To Boudicca!' insisted Mark.

In the silence Desmond burped again. A moorhen scuttled and clucked, dabbing away somewhere on the surface of the lake. 'Spooky,' said Mark, 'Spook!' they both giggled at the childish word. 'A pee. Must have a pee,' said Mark opening the zip of his trousers, struggling with the heavy, wet cloth.

'Sacrilege,' said Desmond wagging his finger that was numb to the knuckle, 'Turn your back man, I'm the captain now.'

Mark turned away, the sound of his urine clear in the silence on and on.

'And mind your boots!' said Desmond but his advice went out like a match as another sound, a woosh, woosh, came out of the darkness, and something rushed, woosh, woosh, towards them and Desmond rolled out of the way and didn't like it. He remembered the woosh and Mark bent now, stooping to do his zip as Boyle appeared beneath the black flapping plastic.

He screamed as he ran towards the two of them, Mark almost bent double, Desmond rolling away, stumbling to get up, get up, from the ground. Woosh, woosh came Boyle with the sabre in his hand, Mark fell hard against the stone, the sabre quivered in the grass. For a moment there was absolute silence, for a moment until Desmond heard beyond the pounding of his heart, his brother's panting breath. Desmond crawled a pace, and then another pace, he vomited into the grass. His hair was covered, he shivered uncontrollably.

'Come on,' said Boyle coming towards him.

Desmond got up on shaky legs. The sabre glinted in the moonlight but there was no blood. The soldier was out cold. 'Jesus! Jesus Christ!' said Desmond and leant against the stone, God Almighty! 'I thought you meant business just then.'

'I do.'

'You don't,' they were whispering.

'I do Desmond, I do. There's a gun in his breast pocket, take it.'

'Take it?' whispered Desmond.

'Take it out.'

Desmond felt the sodden jacket with shaking fingers. His fingers found the gun, 'What?' he whispered.

'Shoot him in the head.'

'In the head,' repeated Desmond.

'In the head.'

Desmond slid slowly down the stone beside the slumped body of the soldier. Boyle stood above him, the sabre in his hand. Clouds, as if pre-arranged, no longer had the grace to cover anything. It was a moonlit night in August, clear as a fucking bell.

Desmond raised the gun, heavy in his hand, his hand hardly fit to hold it. Pressed it to the temple of the stunned man, veering off again, his hand now shaking violently, vomit on his face and in his hair, and ears, vomit on the sleeve of his coat. Boyle placed his hand on his brother's and steadied the gun, together they shot him in the head making a small and perfect hole from which blood issued slowly, red.

Together they dragged him, a body now, limp and hopeless from the stone, over the railings, down among the tight-faced flowers to the shore. Boyle brought out baling twine and they weighted the body with stones. Stones in the zip up pockets of the jacket, stones inside the trouser legs, stones wrapped in the sweater and the Van Heusen shirt, stones about the neck, the wrists, the waist and ankles. They humped the body into the bottom of the boat where it lay sluiced with water, Boyle retrieved the oar, which sweet fortune, remained exactly where it had floated to in a patch of reeds.

Boyle rowed the heavy boat out, out, into the centre of the lake. 'Now,' he said. Very slowly they engineered the corpse into a standing position. Boyle with the oars safely shipped standing in the bow, Desmond kneeling in the water at the bottom of the boat, holding hard to the back of the man's knees.

'Now,' said Boyle, 'Topple him. Shove him hard.'

Desmond shoved and the man fell, the boat lurched as water poured over the gunnel and washed over Desmond who scrambled for his balance.

'Push again, shove,' commanded Boyle for the man's knees sagged over, his feet hooked on the gunnel. 'Push now, quickly!' Desmond heaved, the body went in, the gun after him.

Desmond lay prone and panting in the bow as Boyle took up the oars once more, turning the boat back towards Ballyross. All was silent except for the splashing of the oars, the dip in and out of the water, the phosphorescence catching in the moonlight, the moonlight glinting on the sabre that lay across the thwart.

Boyle pulled slowly home his arms unaccustomed to the oars. Desmond opened his eyes recovering his normal breathing and watched him, his elder brother, from the bow.

'Would you like a little Yeats?' Boyle whispered.

'Surely,' Desmond whispered back and Boyle recited:

'I will arise and go now, and go to Innisfree
And a small cabin build there, of clay and wattles made:
Nine bean-rows will I have there, a hive for the honey-bee,
And live alone in the bee-loud glade.
And I shall have some peace there, for peace comes dropping slow,
Dropping from the veils of the morning to where the cricket sings;
There midnight's all a glimmer, and noon a purple glow,
And evening full of the linnet's wings.'

His voice was quiet and beautiful in the darkness punctuated by the gentle splash as they rowed slowly home and Desmond's voice, the voice without the accent, joined his brother's in the last and perfect stanza:

'I will arise and go now, for always night and day
I hear lake water lapping with low sounds by the shore;
While I stand on the roadway, or on the pavements grey,
I hear it in the deep heart's core.'

Also Available in Pavanne:

Two important novels by Susan Fromberg Schaeffer
Anya and **The Madness of a Seduced Woman**

Susan Fromberg Schaeffer is a well-known American author and poet. She was born in Brooklyn, New York. She was educated in New York City public schools and at the University of Chicago where she received her Ph.D degree in 1966 (and where she wrote the first doctoral dissertation on Vladimir Nabokov). She has written many scholarly articles and is a frequent book reviewer for the Chicago Sun Times. She is Professor of English at Brooklyn College and a founding member of its Master of Arts program in Poetry. She lives in Brooklyn and Vermont with her husband and two children.

Anya is one of the most important novels to be written on the horror of survival in the holocaust. The book grew out of a chance remark made to Susan Fromberg Schaeffer by a survivor of the Nazi concentration camps. '*I was so struck by the cruelty she described that I becme obsessed with what really went on.*' She tracked down survivors and collected all the details she could about life before, during and after the war. The result is a novel of huge scope in the tradition of the great Russian novels, as the New York Times Book Review said, 'a truimph of realism in art'.

Anya tells the story of Anya Savikin, a Russian Jewess who grows up in Poland, between the wars – a time of piano lessons, elaborate meals, country dachas, fancy dress balls, marriages and deaths. All this is swept away by World War II and the firestorm of the holocaust. Anya loses her mother, her father and her husband – only she and her daughter survive.

Since it was first published in America in 1974, *Anya* has sold over two million copies and the author still receives letters from holocaust survivors who have been moved by the book.

'*Anya* is a myth, an epic, the creation of darkness and of laughter stopped forever in the open throat. Out of blown-away dust Susan Fromberg Schaeffer has created a world. It is a vision, set down by a fearless, patient poet . . . a writer of remarkable power'   THE WASHINGTON POST

The Madness of a Seduced Woman

'Striking . . . memorable . . . a most remarkable book' FAY WELDON

'A great many women have tried to write *the* feminist novel . . . *this* is the novel they've been trying to write' MARGARET FORSTER

'DURING ALL THOSE YEARS WHEN EVERYONE WANTED ME TO TELL THEM . . . HOW I CAME TO FIRE THAT SHOT, I NEVER WANTED TO TALK. NOW I THINK I DO . . .'

So begins the story of Agnes Dempster, a beautiful young woman destined to be severely wronged by life and love, whose dreams, thoughts and actions propel her towards a horrific crime of passion she is incapable of preventing.

In her search for an all-consuming, perfect love, Agnes turns her back on an unhappy childhood in Vermont, only to become infatuated with a man who will never make her happy, a betrayer who unwittingly pushes Agnes to the brink of madness, *the madness of a seduced woman* . . .

Set at the turn of the century and inspired by an actual case, *The Madness of a Seduced Woman* is a rich, complex, passionate novel, a powerful evocation of a woman's psyche and the healing and destroying powers of love.

'Fascinating . . . a novel of passion and violence' COMPANY

'The power of this passionate novel lies in the creation of its hero, Agnes. I can't remember a single other character in fiction with whom I have ever identified more' MARGARET FORSTER

'This book asserts the importance of women's feelings, not just this woman's but that of others dedicated to the object of love' FINANCIAL TIMES

Joyce Carol Oates
Solstice

A departure in theme as well as style for this formidable and compelling author, **Solstice** is a novel of obsession – like **The Madness of a Seduced Woman** or **The French Lieutenant's Woman**, only in this case it is the story of a friendship between two women, a manipulative bond of powerful attraction and its sometimes frightening consequences.

It is about Sheila Trask, a famous painter, widow of an even more famous artist who has left her a big house in rural Pennsylvania – and about a younger woman, Monica, a 'golden girl' with golden hair, who has come to teach at a nearby boys' school, recovering from the break-up of her marriage.

'By the end, the two women have undergone the journey to self-knowledge that is the hero's traditional work. The voyage is not for the faint of heart and neither is this book, written in Miss Oates's highly coloured but firmly controlled prose.

'Miss Oates makes us take Monica and Sheila's love–hate bond seriously by creating two believable, complicated women and by grounding her story in the universal.

'Almost half a century ago, Virginia Woolf called for a new kind of fiction, one in which women would be described not "only in relation to the other sex". She predicted that when a woman finally wrote a novel in which "two women are represented as friends" she would "light a torch in that vast chamber where nobody has yet been". Joych Carol Oates, never squeamish about looking into the dark places of the soul, has aimed a powerful beam into that shadowy chamber. *Solstice* should dispel a lot of comforting ideas about the nature of women.'   NEW YORK TIMES REVIEW OF BOOKS

'There is no doubt about one's *living through* Joyce Carol Oates's new book, being submerged by it, becoming one with it. It is a *tour de force*.

'Every subtle nuance of this friendship is chronicled with perception and compassion. The writing is superb, the narrative flow strong and the dialogue memorable.

'But the final touch of genius is the creation of Sheila Trask. Neither Monica nor the reader learns very much about her past or her origins, yet Miss Oates manages to make us feel deeply involved in her strident and disconcerting persona and to accept her – one of the most difficult tasks for a novelist – as a painter of great talent'   DAILY TELEGRAPH

Elizabeth Arthur
Beyond the Mountain

This is an extraordinary combination of fiercely passionate writing about an intense emotional relationship and stunning, vivid descriptive travel writing.

Beyond the Mountain is the story of a woman mountaineer whose husband and brother have recently been killed in an avalanche. With them she formed a world-famous trio of mountain climbers. Now, in an attempt to get over what has happened, she joins an all-women expedition in the Himalayas and interspersed with gruelling experience of the ascent, which incorporates some extraordinary writing about mountaineering, she is forced to come to terms with the past, her grief, and ultimately the fact that her marriage was an extremely difficult one.

The action is played out against the snow-capped peaks of the Himalayas and the stark reality of that horizon contrasts emphatically with the woman's confusion regarding her dead brother and husband.

'Elizabeth Arthur does something very special in her writing: she handles brutal realism and finely crafted fiction as one medium. The background to her story is thoroughly researched. One can hear the crunch of her feet in the snow, feel the cold and battle with her at the same time in the complex realm of emotions. She deals with desire, fear, guilt and love with compelling honesty, painting them in strong primary colours and skipping the pastel hues – but she also manages to be poetic and all the way through, the balance between physical and emotional drama is beautifully achieved. She never goes over the top' LUCY IRVINE, author of *Castaway*

'For myself as a traveller, I particularly appreciated her vividly evocative descriptions of the Nepalese scene. The novel blends a matter-of-fact earthiness with the emotional turmoil of a distressed person, set against a background of mountain climbing – lucid and incisive, with sensitive insights into character relationships' CHRISTINA DODWELL, author of *In Papua New Guinea*

'A densely woven, ambitious book. Its concerns and characters, its lyricism and sculpted form will speak to and impress the sensitive reader . . . Uniquely memorable' THE WASHINGTON POST

'Outstanding . . . clearly a writer of considerable talent' THE NEW YORK TIMES

'The story is as stunning – as stark and subtle – as the blue-and-white landscape that enchants these people' THE NEW YORKER

Sara Maitland
Virgin Territory

Rape: a traumatic experience for any woman, a particular crisis for a nun. Sister Kitty's rape affects all the members of her South American community. She survives. But Sister Anna comes close to a nervous breakdown and it is suggested that she should take a year's sabbatical to recover.

So Sister Anna is sent to London, where she becomes involved in a very different kind of life. Her time is spent studying in the British Library, and helping a couple with their brain-damaged child. Then she meets Karen, a gay feminist, who introduces Anna to a new world, new ideas and new values. For the first time in her life – in her mid-thirties – she is independent, free to listen and to choose. She finds herself in turn excited, challenged, threatened, and eventually forced to reassess her own vocation: what, in the face of rape, and the changing roles of women, can her virginity mean now?

The subject of Sara Maitland's second novel is powerful and she writes boldly, richly and evocatively. With her first novel, *Daughter of Jerusalem*, she won the Somerset Maugham Award. Her short stories have equally received high critical acclaim. Now *Virgin Territory* confirms that she is one of the most talented and original writers to emerge from the British women's movement.

'A challenging and joyful book by an extraordinarily gifted writer'   BOOKS AND BOOKMEN

'The pressures on Anna are extreme – bullying voices of the Church Fathers in her head, the destructive empathy with a brain-damaged child she cares for, and the temptation of physical love with another woman . . . This closely argued polemical novel contains some striking truths that are not often aired'   DAILY TELEGRAPH